Other books by D.R. Graham:

What Are the Chances? (Britannia Beach Series)
And Then What? (Britannia Beach Series)
Rank
One Percenter (Noir et Bleu MC Series)
The Handler (Noir et Bleu MC Series)
It Is What It Is (Noir et Bleu MC Series)
The Noir et Bleu (Noir et Bleu MC Series)
Hit That And You're Dead

Put It Out There

Britannia Beach

D.R. GRAHAM

A division of HarperCollins*Publishers*
www.harpercollins.co.uk

Harper*Impulse* an imprint of
HarperCollins*Publishers*
1 London Bridge Street
London SE1 9GF

www.harpercollins.co.uk

A Paperback Original 2016

First published in Great Britain in ebook format by Harper*Impulse* 2016

Set in Minion by Palimpsest Book Production Ltd, Falkirk, Stirlingshire

Printed and bound in Great Britain

MIX
Paper from
responsible sources
FSC™ C007454

FSC™ is a non-profit international organisation established to promote
the responsible management of the world's forests. Products carrying the
FSC label are independently certified to assure consumers that they come
from forests that are managed to meet the social, economic and
ecological needs of present and future generations,
and other controlled sources.

Find out more about HarperCollins and the environment at
www.harpercollins.co.uk/green

For Morgan

CHAPTER ONE

Summer was officially over, and even though all the families who spent their vacation at the Inn had packed up and gone home, the dining room was crowded for our famous homemade breakfast buffet. Thirty-six guests, all excited for a week-long wilderness retreat. It was our first corporate booking, and I was feeling pretty impressed with myself, since they found us through the new Britannia Beach Inn website I developed for my granddad. He originally hadn't wanted the Inn to have an online presence because he didn't have the staff to handle more guests. We needed the extra revenue to afford repairs on the hundred-and-thirty-year-old building, though. When I made the decision to move back to Britannia and promised to help out before and after school, he finally gave me the go-ahead.

Fully aware of how late it was getting, I sped to restock the pastry basket with warm cinnamon buns and poured fresh-brewed coffee for a table of non-outdoorsy-looking women, decked out in expensive hiking gear. It was already seven-thirty. The only bus from Britannia Beach to Squamish in the morning stopped in front of the Inn at seven forty-two. I needed to catch it if I wanted to make it to school. As I rushed to clear another stack of dirty dishes from a table, my granddad stepped up to the buffet table and scooped fresh scrambled eggs into a warming tray. "You better get going, sweetheart. You don't want to miss the bus."

"You mean, you don't want me to miss the bus."

He chuckled. "True. I am a little too busy to drive you into Squamish today."

I kissed his cheek and removed my apron. "I'm going."

"Don't forget the meeting with the real-estate agent is at five o'clock today if you want to be here."

"Oh." I stopped and spun around, surprised. "I thought you were going to cancel that."

As he stirred the pot of oatmeal with more attention than it needed, he glanced up to gauge my reaction, which he likely knew wasn't going to be supportive. "I want to hear what he has to say."

"Why? If I can keep attracting corporate retreat bookings, you'll start making a profit again."

"That's a big *if*, Derian. I appreciate all the work you've done on the website, and I couldn't have run things around here all summer if you hadn't moved back, but you only have two more years of high school. I need to plan for when you leave for university. There's no harm in hearing what he has to say."

No harm? Except that living with my mom in Vancouver had been a disaster, and I had nowhere else to live, and selling the only place that still held good memories of my dad was something I couldn't deal with on top of all that. "What if it gets bought by a company that just tears it down and redevelops the entire village?"

"There might be a buyer who will renovate the Inn and keep the heritage houses in the village."

I glanced at the yellowed antique clock again. I needed to leave, but I also desperately wanted to talk him out of the meeting before I left. "We can renovate it just as easily as someone else."

He sighed and seemed hesitant to break it to me, "It's too expensive."

2

I swept my arm through the air for emphasis. "Look at how busy we are. Our corporate retreat clients will generate extra income in the off season."

"This is the one and only corporate booking we've had. We have to explore our options. Sorry, sweetheart." He turned, holding the empty pancake tray, and retreated into the kitchen.

He was right, but I wished he wasn't. Deflated, I turned and headed through the lobby. My bedroom was on the first floor at the end of the hall. I zig-zagged past the guest rooms, trying to avoid the floorboards that creaked—not that it mattered since my door squeaked loudly enough to be heard back in the dining room.

To be perfectly honest, my bedroom was one of the many rooms that needed to be renovated, or torn down. Only one of the outlets worked, the window didn't stay open without something propping it up, and the wallpaper was faded and curled at the seams. My bathroom was in even worse shape than my bedroom. The toilet handle didn't work and could only be flushed by pulling on the rusted chain. The tiles on the wall occasionally fell off the plaster and smashed into the rusted claw-foot tub. And the hot water was only hot about thirty percent of the time. Everything was the same as it had been when my mom was growing up. It was hard to imagine it any other way. But when I actually took notice, it was kind of impossible to ignore the fact that it was run down.

Trying to forget about the potential sale, I scrubbed my face and brushed my teeth. Unfortunately, my hair had to stay hanging boringly down my back in waves since there wasn't enough time to straighten it. After tossing my yoga pants and Britannia Beach Inn polo shirt into the hamper, I dressed in a skirt, sweater and boots, and grabbed my canvas school bag. Without pausing to look in the mirror, I left out of the side emergency exit door next to my bedroom and jogged across the parking lot towards the highway and the bus stop.

Before I reached the shoulder of the highway, the bus blew by. I raced along the gravel, arms waving. But the driver didn't see me, or didn't care.

"Great," I mumbled. There was nobody to cover for my granddad during the time it would take to drive me into town. School wasn't going to happen. Not a good start to starting over. Maybe there was no point in going back, period. If the Inn went up for sale, it didn't make sense to go back to school after a year away, only to move again.

My eighteen-year-old next-door neighbour Trevor stepped off his porch and leaned against the side of his 4Runner, watching my mopey walk with an amused look on his face. We hadn't seen each other since the end of June because he'd been away travelling in South America on a motorbike all summer. He looked extra rugged, but still like himself in his standard white T-shirt and dark jeans. "Need a ride?"

I honestly wanted to go back to my room and curl up under the covers. My granddad would probably insist on leaving the guests unattended and driving me himself, though, so I said, "Yeah, I guess so." I walked across the lot to where he was parked and reached up to hug him. "Welcome home."

"You too." He squeezed his arms and wrapped me in a warmth that did feel like home, but it reminded me that Britannia Beach might not be my home for long. I stepped back and tucked my hair behind my ears as I glanced at our tiny old mining village— twelve heritage houses, a small diner, a church, and a couple of tourist shops—backed up against the base of the forested mountain and across the highway from the beach. It was quaint, but old and easy to miss.

Not wanting to think about the fate of the village, I focused back on the immediate problem. "I don't want you to make a special trip into town just for me. Were you headed into Squamish anyway?"

"Yup. I picked up a shift at the docks. And Kailyn needs a ride

4

to her program." He reached over to take my school bag and placed it in the back of the truck.

"Thank you. My granddad thanks you, too."

"No problem."

"How was your motorcycle trip?"

He eyed my outfit with an expression that was difficult to read. A skirt and boots were a change for me compared to the tomboyish ponytail, jeans, and bulky sweaters I normally wore. I wanted to make a statement at school that I wasn't the same quiet, boring Derian they had known before I moved away. Based on Trevor's reaction, it wasn't producing the statement I had hoped for. "The trip was good," he finally answered.

"Why are you looking at me funny?"

"I'm not. You look nice," he said, but it sounded more like he was just being polite.

I ran my hand down the side of the beige skirt my mom bought during one of her attempts to make me more urban chic. "Do you think the skirt's too short?"

He grinned as if I'd cracked a joke.

Embarrassed that he thought my attempt to reinvent myself was humorous, I mumbled, "Never mind," then changed the subject. "I didn't know you were back. You could have come over for breakfast."

"I was going to, but we got home late last night. The jet lag made me sleep through my alarm."

I nodded, distracted by the years of memories of our families eating breakfast together at the Inn. Growing up, Trevor and I used to always play together, but after he went to high school, the only time we ever really hung out was with our dads and his sister at breakfast. We hadn't eaten breakfast together since before my dad's accident, and I suddenly realized how much I missed it—another one of the many things that came to an abrupt end when my dad died.

As if Trevor could read my mind, he reached over with one

5

arm and hugged me into his chest. He didn't say anything. He didn't need to. He knew how close I had been to my dad, and he knew how my world imploded after the accident. Although his familiarity was comforting, I stepped back to end the hug. My grief was surfacing, and I didn't want it to. Everyone at school knew why I had moved away for a year. The stares and whispers were going to be hard enough to face without also being an emotional wreck at the same time.

Trevor checked my expression to make sure I was okay, then shoved my shoulder in a playful way to get me to smile. "You can make me breakfast tomorrow. Kiki, let's get a move on," he called back towards the house at his sister. She was born with Down syndrome and, although she was older than him, Trevor had been helping to take care of her since their mom took off. He opened the front passenger door for me as Kailyn stepped out onto the porch of their house and locked the door with the key she wore around her neck. "Are you getting in?" Trevor asked me.

"Kailyn likes the front seat. I'll sit in the back."

He stepped forward and opened the back door for me before he walked around and hopped into the driver's seat. Kailyn climbed into the front passenger seat and slammed the door. She clicked her seatbelt on, tucked her straight blonde bob behind her ears, and opened one of the pre-teen magazines she was crazy about, even though she was nineteen. Her freshly applied lip balm made the air smell like the Strawberry Shortcake doll I played with when I was little.

"Hi, Kailyn," I said as Trevor pulled out of the Inn's parking lot and turned north on the Sea-to-Sky highway to head to Squamish.

Kailyn didn't say hi back, but she asked without looking up from the magazine, "Did you know that Austin Sullivan's favourite thing to eat is Hawaiian pizza? And his birthday is on April seventeenth?"

"No. I don't even know who Austin Sullivan is," I answered, never really that up on trends.

"Gah!" She slammed the magazine down in her lap exaggeratedly. "Deri. You're so silly. Everyone knows who Austin Sullivan is. He sings the song that goes, '*When I see your eyes, eyes, eyes, I want to cry, cry, cry.*' You know." She sang in her husky monotone voice. I didn't recognize the song at all.

Trevor looked over his shoulder at me and smiled because my face obviously showed my utter ignorance of pop culture. He joined in and sang the lyrics with Kailyn. "Recognize it now?" he asked me with a wink.

"No. Let me see his picture. Maybe I'll recognize him." I leaned forward to peek over Kailyn's shoulder. She showed me a magazine page with a collage of twenty different teen idols. I had no idea which one was him, so I said, "Oh yeah, he's really cute."

"He looks like my brother, don't you think?"

"Really?" I sat forward. "Show me again. Which one is he?"

She held the magazine up and pointed to a ruggedly handsome outdoorsy-type guy who had dark hair and light eyes. He was on a farm, shirtless, with a cut chest and abs, leaning up against a wood fence. He did look like Trevor. I sat back in my seat and Kailyn grinned wide enough that her chubby, freckled cheeks made her eyes squint shut. "Deri thinks Austin Sullivan is really cute, and he looks just like you. That means she thinks you're really cute. Did you know that?"

Trevor didn't turn his head, but I could see his eyes in the rearview mirror. They darted for a second to look at me.

Kailyn turned in her seat to face me. "You and Trevor should get married one day," she whispered loudly.

Right. As if that would ever happen. Trevor could have any girl he wanted, and the introverted tomboy next door wasn't even on the list. He smiled—maybe because the idea of getting married to someone he thought of as a kid sister was ridiculous, or maybe because he couldn't wait to tease me for saying a guy who looks

7

like him is cute. Either way, the entire topic of conversation made me uncomfortable. Fortunately, one of Austin Sullivan's songs came on the radio. Kailyn turned the radio up, and we drove along the winding highway without talking.

The road followed the coastline with the ocean on our left and the mountain rock faces to our right. It was one of the most pristine places on earth to live. I definitely didn't want to have to leave it behind again. When we arrived at the community centre for adults with disabilities, Trevor turned the radio volume down and whistled through his teeth to break Kailyn's attention from her magazine. "We're here."

She climbed out of the truck without saying thanks or goodbye and slammed the door. Her wide strides made her stocky body sway from side to side. After she disappeared inside the building, Trevor looked over his shoulder at me. I thought he was going to embarrass me for the Austin Sullivan comparison. Instead, he asked, "Aren't you going to get in the front?"

"Oh yeah, right." I jumped out of the truck and hopped into the front passenger seat.

As he pulled out of the community centre's parking lot and headed back onto the highway, a bizarre image flicked through my mind: *a girl's head smashed against the ground, and her blonde hair turned red from the blood pooled on the floor.*

Trevor glanced at me, concerned, as he waited for me to tell him what I saw. I didn't want to. My meaningless intuition visions, inherited from grandmother's grandmother, started when I was about three. Back then, I'd see things like a dish fall off the counter before it actually did, or I'd point to where the whales were going to breach long before they showed up. When I was little, I thought everyone could see things before they happened. I was shocked when Trevor told me he couldn't. He used to play games with me to test if I could guess what card he was holding or what picture he drew, but I always failed. The intuition never worked on demand like that. It wasn't something I could will. Instead, I would randomly show up at his house wearing my full snowsuit and toque and mitts, ready for the storm that wasn't forecasted. He'd look up at the blue sky and bright sunshine, sceptical, but he trusted me enough to go back inside to put his snowsuit on too.

Being able to see things in advance started to bother me when I was about nine because the scattered visions and subtle senses began to only happen for upsetting things. I once had a dream the neighbour's dog was going to get hit by a car, so I sat outside their yard all day to make sure he didn't get out. I was really proud of myself for saving him until it happened a week later. It was frustrating to not know when it would happen, and I felt so guilty. When I was twelve, I had a vision that my grandmother got sick and died in the hospital. Three weeks after the vision, she was diagnosed with cancer. She died a year later.

After I saw my dad's car accident happen, I attempted to block all my intuitions. I promised myself the new Derian would no longer have visions. Unfortunately, despite determined effort on my part, I couldn't stop them.

"What did you see?" Trevor asked.

I should have known he wouldn't let me off the hook. "Nothing. It was a headache."

He frowned and focused on the road. "I've known you most of your life. I know what it means when you get that look on your face. You don't have to pretend you don't get premonitions. It's me."

"They aren't premonitions. They're useless images, like crazy dreams. It was nothing. Nothing that makes any sense."

"They aren't useless. Search and Rescue teams are helped by intuitive and clairvoyant people all the time. While I was in Peru, I met a woman who finds missing children. I told her about you. She recommended I read her book. She says people with natural intuition can practice and get better at it, just like any other skill. I brought it home for you to read."

I opened my bag and dug through it, hoping there was something I could use as a distraction to avoid the conversation. There wasn't anything. "Why would I want to get good at seeing traumatic things I can't do anything about?"

"The better you get at it, the more likely it will be useful. Maybe you'll save someone's life someday."

I slouched in the seat and crossed my arms over my chest, fixing my attention on the rock face next to the highway. "A lot of good it did my dad. I saw it happen in exact, excruciating detail and couldn't prevent it. He still died."

Trevor glanced at me with empathy in his eyes. "Your dad's accident wasn't your fault, Deri."

I shrugged and fought to swallow down the emotion in my throat. "Either way, I want to practice not having intuition at all, not practice to get better at it."

We drove in silence. He probably wanted to convince me my brain glitch was a huge asset, but fortunately he let it go. "How are you feeling about being back at school in Squamish?"

Thankful to talk about anything other than my flawed neurology, I said, "Excited and nervous, I guess. It will be awkward at first when they all try to be sensitive about my dad. Hopefully that won't last long and everything goes back to normal." As soon as I said it, I regretted using the word "normal". My life was never going back to the way it was. It was never going to feel normal again. I exhaled, trying to steel myself for the day ahead.

"It's going to be okay."

In an attempt to lighten the mood, I joked, "Yeah. Anything is better than living with my mom."

A deep crease etched between his eyebrows. "She's not that bad," he said quietly.

Before my dad died, my mom lived in our apartment in downtown Vancouver and only came up to Britannia on the weekends, which was great growing up. Living full-time with my dad at the Inn had worked perfectly since he and I were essentially the same person—nature-lovers, bookish, and artistic. The opposite of my mom. Since Trevor's mom left them, he always thought I should appreciate the fact that I, at least, had a mom, even if she and I had nothing in common. My whole childhood, he had encouraged me to try harder to get along with her.

I knew I needed to get over my issues with my mom, especially after losing my dad. I just didn't know how. After my dad died, my mom refused to drive on the highway between Vancouver and Britannia, where the accident happened. She acted like it was a panic attack thing, but I knew it was just her convenient excuse to never step foot in Britannia Beach again and to guilt me into moving to Vancouver.

I tried to make living with her work. I really did. I enrolled in the stuffy private school she had always wanted me to go to. I joined the clubs she thought would look good on my university applications. I attended the counselling sessions she insisted on, so I could "process my grief". None of it made any difference. I missed my friends in Squamish, I missed my granddad, and most of all I missed Britannia Beach. My mom and I got on each other's nerves. Her standards for everything were impossibly high, she worried so much it was suffocating, and I hated every minute of living in the loud, crowded city. Moving back to the Inn saved me. And I wasn't sure I could survive losing it too.

Trevor and I didn't talk for the rest of the drive, which was something I actually always appreciated about him. He was comfortable with quiet, like my dad. And like me. But his silence felt different, more serious. As if something had changed between us in the year I was gone. He didn't even look at me again until we pulled up in front of my school and shifted into park.

Things still felt odd between us. I wasn't sure how to handle it and ended up sounding awkwardly formal. "Thank you for the ride, Trevor. Have a good day."

"I'll be done work at four-thirty if you want a ride home."

"Sure. I'll meet you back here."

11

After I stepped out and shut the door, the window rolled down.

"Hey." He grinned with his chin tilted in a cocky way. "Do you really think I'm good-looking like that guy in Kailyn's magazine?"

And there it was. We were back to normal. The teasing was going to be relentless. I shook my head and made a snarky face. "Don't let it go to your gigantic head."

"Too late." He waved and drove away.

At least our relationship felt familiar and easy again. Which was good, since I had a feeling going back to my old school was going to be way harder than I had anticipated.

CHAPTER TWO

My best friend Sophie Sakamoto wasn't hard to spot in her black-and-white-striped knee-high stockings, black micro-mini skirt, and fluorescent lime-green tank top. She lounged on the front steps of the school with her boyfriend and some of the guys from their band. Her boyfriend Doug was in grade twelve and they'd been dating for almost two years. They came down to Vancouver almost every weekend to hang out with me when I lived there, thankfully. The loneliness would have been unbearable if they hadn't. Doug had shaved his dark faux-hawk into a buzz cut since I last saw him. It suited the dark-rimmed punk glasses he wore. Most people got the wrong impression about Doug because he was a musician who wore leather and had tattoos up his neck—well, maybe it wasn't entirely the wrong impression.

"Hey, guys," I said, loud enough for them to hear me, but quietly enough to not make a huge scene. At least, that was the goal. I should have known Sophie wouldn't let my re-initiation to the school slide without a bit of a scene.

She shot up and squealed as she lunged over to hug me. "Oh my God. Welcome back. You are not allowed to leave me ever again. The boredom was torture." She turned to the boys. "No offence."

They all laughed, knowing full well it was intended to be an insult. She leaned back to check out my outfit. Normally, she was the one up on fashion, and I couldn't have cared less. The suede boots were one of the expensive items my mom had bought for me while I was living with her.

"Damn, Derian, you look stylish." She tickled my waist. "All we need now is to get you a boyfriend."

I glared at her and whispered, "I'm happily single. Thanks. You want to keep your voice down a little? Please."

"Why are you turning all red?" she teased. She was going to take it as far as she could, just to amuse herself. And maybe also to get back at me for leaving her alone for a whole year. "Hey, Doug," Sophie called over to him. "You think Derian looks hot with her new look?"

Doug laughed. "Is that a trap?"

"Nope."

To my horror, Doug and a couple of other guys on the steps all checked me out. Doug pushed his glasses up, studied my suede boots, then moved his gaze up my legs, over my skirt, paused for a second at my pink button-up sweater, and finished at my face. "Yup," he said.

"Smokin'," another guy added.

"See," Sophie encouraged.

I turned sideways and folded my arms across my chest. "You can stop humiliating me. I'm sorry I left you for a year. It's not like I wanted to."

Her expression changed into sympathy before she hugged me again. "I understand why you didn't come back last year. I'm not mad at you, and I wasn't kidding. You look beautiful. But you've always been beautiful—even in worn yoga pants and muddy hiking boots."

"Thank you." I sighed and tugged down the hem of my skirt. It wasn't about the clothes. The look was only supposed to be symbolic of a fresh new start. I thought a new image would help

14

me move on and leave the pain of losing my dad in the past. I hadn't done it to please my mom, or get attention, or pretend to be someone I wasn't, but if it was going to seem like that, I would prefer for everyone to treat me like the old Derian and pretend like nothing had changed. The only problem was, everything had changed. And it had nothing to do with how I dressed.

Sophie slapped my hand to make me stop fidgeting. Then she gasped, dug her fingers into my arms, and spun me around. A guy I'd never seen before closed the driver's door of a black Mercedes coupe. He ran his left hand through his caramel-coloured hair as he turned to look at the school. Then he lifted the tan leather strap of his bag over his head, adjusted it across his chest, and glanced at all the students milling around on the grass and the front steps. "Holy shit. Who is that?" Sophie whispered.

I didn't respond. I just watched him. He walked smoothly and confidently for a few steps, then looked down at the ground for a step—as if what he was doing was the last thing he wanted to be doing. His grey trousers, light blue-grey shirt, and expensive-looking black dress shoes were not the typical look for our high school. His skin was tanned like he'd just gotten back from the south of France or something, and his shiny silver watch must have cost a fortune. When he got close enough that I could tell he was over six-feet tall, and his eyes were the most intoxicating shade of blue, he smiled. It was a shy smile. His chin was down, but he glanced up briefly before flashing his insanely white and perfectly straight teeth at Sophie.

She and I both stared at him as he continued towards the front door of the school and disappeared inside. "He's beautiful." Sophie sighed.

"And he smiled at you," I whispered, as I checked to see if Doug was listening. He wasn't paying attention.

"He didn't smile at me, you geek." Sophie smacked my arm with the back of her hand. "He smiled at you."

"No, he didn't."

"Ya, he did. I'll get the 411 on him for you." She jiggled around excitedly.

"What? No. I don't want you to do that."

"Hi Derian," a male voice interrupted us before I had a chance to axe her scheme.

I jumped a little because I hadn't even noticed Steve Rawlings walk up. He was a friend who sat on student council with me the year before I left. He looked different. He'd grown about six inches and got his braces off. His hair was cut really short—probably because it was the first day of school. He was kind of a keener like that. He actually looked cute.

"Hi Steve."

"Welcome back, Deri. Are you coming to peer mentoring?"

"Oh, I didn't sign up to be a mentor."

"I know, but I remembered you said you wanted to be a mentor in junior year. So, when I heard you were coming back, I signed you up. Hope that's okay. Mr. Orton said he was going to send you an email. Sorry. He must have forgotten. I would have told you, but I don't have your email or phone number. It's cool if you have other things you need to do."

"I did, I mean, I do want to be a mentor. Yeah, thanks."

Sophie grabbed my elbow to hold me back. "She'll be right with you," she said to Steve, then whispered in my ear, "I'll fill you in on the new guy by lunch."

"What? No. Don't embarrass me," I hissed back.

She giggled in a maniacal way, held up two fingers in a peace sign, and moved to lean against Doug. Doug draped his arm over her shoulders and kissed her neck. There wasn't any way to stop her once her mind was set on something, so I didn't bother to protest more before I walked away.

"Do you want me to carry your bag?" Steve offered.

"Oh, it's basically empty. But thanks for asking."

He smiled in a nervous way that made me feel vicariously awkward.

16

It took a while, but I eventually came up with something to say to break the silence. "You grew a lot since I saw you last."

His face winced slightly, maybe wishing I hadn't reminded him he used to be smaller than me. "A bit."

"And have you been working out or something?"

His cheeks definitely went red at that point, which wasn't the effect I was going for. "I've been coaching tennis at the community centre."

"Oh, I didn't know you played."

"I've been on the school tennis team since grade eight." He looked a little hurt that I didn't know.

"Right, I knew that," I scrambled. Truthfully, football was the only sport I paid attention to since it was what Trevor had played in high school.

Steve chuckled, "I was on student council with you too. My name's Steve. Do you at least remember that?"

I squished up my face and squinted exaggeratedly. "You look vaguely familiar," I joked, and we walked into the students' lounge, where the grade eights were all huddled around, chattering.

The chairs were set up in two rows facing each other. Our principal yelled for the mentors to sit along one side. Steve and I sat beside each other and talked as we waited for our buddies to be assigned. A tiny girl with strawberry curls sat down in the chair in front of Steve. She grinned shyly and her cheeks turned pink as if she thought Steve was one of the celebrities in Kailyn's magazine.

"Hi. I'm Steve Rawlings." He reached his arm out and shook her hand.

She scanned the room, as if she hoped her friends could see that she lucked out and got a hot guy as her mentor. My buddy was as small as the girl and even a little skinnier. He had dark hair and very pale skin. His eyes were hard to see because he wore wire-rimmed glasses, and he hadn't looked up since he sat down.

"Hi. I'm Derian. What's your name?"

He glanced up. His eyes were big and brown. He focused back down at his lap and said, with an adorable cartoon-pitched voice, "Nikolai."

"Nice to meet you, Nikolai. Do you have any questions about high school so far?"

His head tilted up, but he didn't speak.

"That's what I'm here for. If you need anything at all, just ask me."

He shook his head—not like he didn't have any questions, more like he was too afraid to ask them.

"When I was in grade eight I wanted to know lots of things." I pulled out the map from his student agenda and showed him where all the important things were. "This is where my locker is." I marked it with a circle on the map. "If you need anything just come find me."

He smiled a little and looked around nervously, as if he expected someone to spring on him or something. At that point, the principal shouted instructions again.

After we walked our buddies to their lockers and pointed them in the right direction for their first classes, I asked Steve, "Were we that cute in grade eight?"

"You were. I definitely wasn't. What's your first class?"

"Um," I opened my binder and read my schedule. "English with Mrs. Tookey."

"Kooky Tookey. Me too. May I have the honour of escorting you to class, Miss Lafleur?" He presented his arm so I could hook my arm around his elbow like a Jane Austen character.

"Certainly, my dear sir."

We sat beside each other halfway down the aisle of desks in Mrs. Tookey's classroom. She really was kooky. She breezed in with a trail of rainbow scarves twisting behind her. Her hair was clumped into long dirty-blonde dreads and tied into a ponytail with a red shoelace. It was a style that matched her long peasant skirt, Birkenstock sandals, and pink socks. I chuckled a little as she took in a deep breath and smiled at us lovingly. "Namaste," she said.

The entire class stared at her, not sure how to respond.

She pressed her palms together in a prayer position and bowed. "All right, before we jump right into work I would like everyone to take a moment to set an intention for this year."

Lisa Alvarez, who acted like a teacher's pet and got away with things because of her looks, shot her hand up and asked, "Intention for what?"

Mrs. Tookey smiled adoringly. "Whatever you wish—the sky is the limit. If you want something to be, just think about it happening. The universe will provide it for you when the timing is right."

Lisa glanced at Steve, he looked at me. A bunch of guys at the back of the class laughed. I could only imagine what types of things they were going to wish for. Steve shot a quick look at the guys behind him and smiled. Then he looked back at me and tried to appear serious again.

"Think of something in this world you wish would become a reality for you," Mrs. Tookey continued. "All right, everyone close your eyes. Rest your feet firmly on the ground. Relax. Feel your breath flow in and out. Think about what you wish would come true for you—something that will bring you supreme happiness. Now put it out there."

The guys at the back snickered again. Mrs. Tookey cleared her throat, annoyed. I thought about what I wanted my intention to be. The only thing I wanted with all my heart was for my dad not to be dead. There weren't enough intentions in the world to make that true. Wishing for my dream car made me seem kind of materialistic since other people had way less than I did. Straight As were achievable without intervention from the universe. Hopefully, getting kissed for the first time was a milestone I could also achieve on my own accord. I clenched my eyes shut and set an intention that meant something: *I will find a way to earn enough money to do the renovations so Granddad will be able to keep the Inn.*

I opened my eyes. Steve stared at me eagerly. "What intention did you set?"

"Isn't it like a wish? If I tell you, it won't come true."

He waved his hand to dismiss my concern. "Nah, the more people you tell, the stronger the intention will become."

"What's yours?"

"That you'll go out with me on Saturday night." He smiled and raised his eyebrows expectantly.

"Oh," I muttered, totally unprepared for that.

His smile faded.

CHAPTER THREE

Thankfully, Mrs. Tookey lectured for the entire class, so Steve and I couldn't finish the conversation about going out on Saturday night. I was not experienced at all in the world of dating. I needed to consult with Sophie before I gave Steve an answer. When Mrs. Tookey dismissed us, Lisa Alvarez grabbed Steve's elbow to ask him a question. She did things like act dumb with guys to have an excuse to flirt, even though her grades were at least as good as mine. I took the opportunity to shoot out of my seat and rushed to disappear into the crowd of people in the hall.

I bit my fingernails through my next two classes, watching the clock impatiently. When lunch finally arrived, I pretty much sprinted to the lounge to check in with Nikolai. He still looked shell-shocked, but he had hooked up with another boy who he must have known from elementary school. They were sort of glued to each other. "How's it going, Nikolai?"

"Um, okay," he said as he glanced at his friend.

I smiled because his cartoon voice was ridiculously cute. "I'll be sitting over there if you need anything." I pointed to the table where I always met Sophie. Then it occurred to me I'd been gone for a year and actually had no idea what Sophie and the guys did for lunch anymore.

"Okay," Nikolai said again, almost as if he was embarrassed I was hovering. He sat down with his friend at a table full of grade eights. Obviously, he didn't need my help. I was the one who needed help. No one was at our old table yet, and Steve had already walked in with his friends. If he cornered me before I had a chance to talk to Sophie, I wouldn't know how to act. Well, that wasn't true. It wasn't rocket science—say yes or no. The problem was, I didn't know which to say.

I almost went back to sit with Nikolai and his grade-eight friends just so I wouldn't be alone. I glanced around the students' lounge, hoping to spot Sophie or Doug. Instead, I saw the new guy walk in surrounded by a bunch of grade-twelve girls, who had obviously offered to show him around and have lunch with him. My nose squished up and my lip curled unintentionally because they were the snottiest girls in our school. He sat down at a table squeezed between Corrine Andrews on his right and Paige Peterson on his left. When he glanced up, our eyes accidentally met, so I quickly stared at the floor. I covered my mouth with my hand in case I still had the snarled-lip thing going on. The next time I checked, he was smiling—I couldn't tell why. Corrine might have said something funny, not that she was known for her wit.

Steve sat at a corner table with a bunch of guys. He scanned the room and stopped at me. My heart raced like a baby gazelle separated from the herd.

"Hey, Derian," Lisa Alvarez said as she put a tray with an apple and water on the table next to me. Her smile and tone weren't exactly genuine when she said, "Welcome back."

"Thanks." When did she start sitting at the table with Sophie and the guys? Had she been my substitute? If they were trying to replace me, I would have preferred if they had chosen someone with a sliver of integrity.

She sat down and said, "I saw your brother drop you off this morning. Is he dating anyone?"

"Trevor's not my brother. He's my neighbour."

22

Surprised, she said, "Really? He acts like he's your brother. Is he single?"

Her eyes were gorgeous, big, with long lashes. And her lips were famous. She'd been every guy's fantasy girl since her figure developed in grade seven. But Trevor didn't date insecure girls, girly girls, or girls younger than him. None that I knew of. Even if Lisa Alvarez miraculously gained self-respect, she didn't have a chance with him. "You're not Trevor's type."

She flipped her long, shiny, brown hair over her shoulders and laughed. "I'm everyone's type."

I couldn't argue with that, if all they were looking for was someone to get lucky with. Thankfully, Sophie, Doug, and the guys from their band had showed up. Sophie leaned in to speak closely to Lisa's face in an intimidating way, "Trevor likes classy girls, Lisa. You haven't got a snowball's chance in hell."

"Why don't we let him be the judge of that?" She bit into her apple and looked pretty cocky.

Sophie pointed and said, "Sit over at that table. Don't make me tell you again."

Unfazed, Lisa stood with an arrogant grin and wandered over to sit with a different group of grade elevens. If Sophie did that to me, I'd be bawling, so either Lisa was made of Teflon, or she was a master at burying the humiliation. I grabbed Sophie's arm and dragged her out of the lounge before she had a chance to cause more trouble.

"Wow, you're eager." Sophie laughed. "Okay, his name is Mason Cartwright. He's in grade twelve and just moved to Squamish from Ottawa. His dad owns some sort of import company, and they're filthy, stinking, disgusting, crazy rich. Apparently his dad commutes to work in a damn helicopter."

"What? That's not what I want to talk about. Wait, how did you find all that out so fast?"

"I called Julie at the hair salon. She gets the low-down on everyone. What did you want to talk about?"

"I think Steve asked me out on a date for this Saturday night."

"You think?"

"He didn't actually ask. We did this thing in English class where you set an intention and put it out there so the universe will make it come true. His intention was that I would go out with him Saturday night."

"What did you tell him?"

"Nothing, yet. Tookey started talking and then I ran out of the classroom before he had a chance to ask for real."

"Well, your answer should be no, simply on the grounds that he used Kooky Tookey's kooky exercise to ask you out." She made a pouty puppy-dog face. "Besides, you have to come to our gig on Saturday night. It's our first real paid show and we need Dirty Deri there."

Oh God, no. Dirty Deri was a one-time thing when I was going through a bad time right after my dad died. I was willing to go to their gig, but Dirty Deri was staying home, locked in a closet. "If I say yes to Steve, I'll insist on going to watch you guys play. I just don't know if I should say yes."

"What is your Spidey-sense intuition telling you?"

"Nothing about boys. But some random girl is going to suffer a head injury, apparently."

"Warn me if she's Japanese. I have no problem rocking a helmet as an accessory."

"She had blonde hair, so unless you have plans to bleach yours out, it wasn't you."

She leaned her back against the wall and crossed her arms as she considered my dilemma. "Do you like Steve?"

"I don't know. He kind of talks a lot, but he's really nice and smart. Apparently he plays on the tennis team."

"And he got cute over the summer," she pointed out.

"Yes, yes he did." I contemplated. "But I want to focus on school. And I promised to help out at the Inn. I don't really have time to date."

24

"Deri, you need to at least kiss a boy before you go to college."

"So, I should say yes?"

"Actually, I think you should wait and see if anything happens with Mason Cartwright."

"Hardly." An involuntary snort caught in my throat from the ridiculousness of that. I needed to crawl before I could qualify for the Olympics. "He's sitting with Corrine and Paige already."

"Don't sell yourself short. Tell Steve you'll go out with him as friends so you can still leave your options open." She patted me on the shoulder and leaned in to add, "And since he's walking over here right now, I'll leave you to that."

My palms immediately got sweaty. Sophie left, and I slowly turned around to face Steve. I couldn't exactly read his expression as he walked along the path with his hands in his pockets, but I assumed it was some variation of insulted. "Hey," he said quietly once we were face to face.

"Hi. Sorry I had to run off after class."

"No problem." He looked into my eyes. "I was wondering—"

I cut him off, "Did you mean you want to go out Saturday night as friends?" I smiled enthusiastically, as if I loved the idea. "Or, did you mean you want to go out on Saturday night for a date?" I wrinkled my nose and angled my eyebrows together to imply I wasn't quite ready for that idea, which was true, so wasn't hard to produce.

He hesitated for a second before he said, "Friends. Maybe we could go to the party Sophie's band is playing at."

"Oh, okay, sure."

"Great." He smiled and handed me a key chain. "I know this is kind of lame, but I went to Arizona over the summer. There is this famous architect place there—"

"Taliesin West."

"Yeah, the Frank Lloyd Wright school. My dad made me go with him for a tour. I remembered when we did that career day in grade eight, you said you wanted to be an architect. And I know you're always sketching buildings, so I thought you might like it. The key chain is the logo or emblem or something."

"Wow. Thanks." I honestly was impressed that he remembered my interest in architecture and was thoughtful enough to get me a souvenir.

"I'm glad you're back. Things weren't the same when you weren't here last year."

Aw, he was being so sweet. "Thanks. It feels good to be home again."

He shifted his weight a couple of times. "Okay, well, um, I have a tennis team meeting, so, I guess I'll see you around."

"Okay, I'll see you around."

He headed towards the gym, and I walked slowly back into the students' lounge, still processing what just happened. A boy asked me out. A cute, smart, super-nice boy, who obviously doesn't mind my geek side. I had never thought of Steve in that way, but then again, I had never really thought of any guy as more than a friend. If there were such a thing as romantically stunted, that was me. Dating was a foreign concept to me. Everything I knew about boys was either from Sophie, who started dating when we were twelve. Or from observing Trevor, who had a different pretty girl hanging around him monthly. I didn't actually have any hands-on experience, but there was no reason why the new Derian couldn't have a boyfriend if I wanted her to.

Sophie sat up with a hopeful look on her face as I approached the table. "So, do you have a date with Steve for Saturday night?"

"As friends. I made that clear, since I'm not at all prepared to jump head first into the deep end of dating."

"Yes! I can't wait to help you choose an outfit." She grinned and clapped her hands in front of her face. "Ooh, let's make this even more interesting," she said in a calculated tone as she stood. Her chair scraped loudly as it slid out behind her.

My mouth literally fell open as she crossed the lounge and leaned her hands on the table Mason was seated at. She spoke directly to him, not even bothering to acknowledge Corrine and Paige. When she pointed her thumb back over her shoulder, Mason glanced at me and smiled. I considered diving under my table. Sophie stood up straight and flipped her long black hair over her shoulders. She shot a look at the girls at the table, but it didn't appear she said anything to them. The last thing she did was gesture at Mason in a see-you-there kind of way and turned to strut back towards our table. I stopped looking at Mason. Mortified.

"God, he's gorgeous," she sighed as she sat back down beside me.

"I. Am. Going. To. Kill. You," I hissed and made a point of articulating each murderess word slowly.

"I didn't even mention you. I just told him about the band. And pointed out that it might be a good place to meet people, you know, since he's new in town."

I shook my head in utter opposition. "You are so dead. When did everything become about getting Derian a date? Let's find a new topic. Music, genetically modified produce, world peace, or—"

"Ah, come on. If having two guys to choose from isn't fun for you, it will at least be entertaining for me to watch."

"I'm so glad my non-existent love life amuses you."

"An existent love life would amuse me more, especially if it's with two guys at once."

"I don't have the time, skill level, or experience to date one guy, let alone two. Fortunately, there's more to life than boys. How about we focus on something other than me finding a mate?"

"I'm not suggesting you go boy crazy, but it won't kill you to take your nose out of a book and get a little action. Guaranteed, your health-class textbook will back me up. Getting busy is a normal, healthy part of adolescent social development." She leaned over and interrupted Doug and his incentive program friends in the middle of a debate about some political conflict.

27

"College guys will prefer a woman who knows what she's doing, right?"

"Yup," he said, without even hesitating. Then it hit him that he probably should have thought about it before he responded. "Was that a trap?"

"Nope," she reassured him and turned back to me. "See. Trust me, my little dating Padawan."

Getting a little action, as she put it, just for the sake of gaining experience, honestly didn't appeal to me. Being the only university student who had never been kissed, however, was not all that appealing either.

CHAPTER FOUR

The rest of the afternoon dragged because, as it turned out, not much had changed in the year I'd been gone. Same boring classes, same small-town teachers, and same shallow, immature class-mates. After school, I walked across the grass to wait for Trevor. Since I didn't have any homework to do and forgot to bring a book, I just sat on a bench next to the parking lot. The day hadn't gone at all how I imagined it would go. A few people had welcomed me back. A few people had no idea who I was. Most people acted as if they hadn't even noticed I'd been missing for a year. Not one person said anything about my dad. It wasn't exactly bad, but it wasn't what I expected either.

Twenty minutes passed before I realized Steve was one of the people playing tennis in the courts in front of me. When he finished his match, or game, or set—whichever it was, he walked over and sat beside me on the bench. "Do you need a ride?"

"No thanks. Trevor is picking me up after he finishes work."

"Oh, is he your boyfriend or something?"

That was a first. People mistook him for my brother all the time, but nobody had ever asked if he was my boyfriend. "No. He's my neighbour."

"So, you don't have a boyfriend?"

x

"No. Do you have a girlfriend?"

"I hope to." He grinned and leaned in a little. "I'm going to set another intention. I'll let you know how it turns out."

Was he flirting? It felt like flirting, not that I was an expert. My face definitely flushed and my stomach felt weird. "Did you have a good practice?" I asked, to break the awkwardness.

"Yeah, I was killing it," he joked. "Weren't you watching?"

Not sure how to admit that although I'd stared right at the tennis courts the entire time, I was thinking about other things and not paying attention. I said, "Sure. You were awesome like, like, um. Who's a famous tennis star?"

He laughed at my unsuccessful attempt to sound athletically hip. "I was awesome like Roger Federer. You can tell everyone you think that."

"Roger Federer. I will, if I can remember his name."

He smiled before he said, "Your hair is such a cool colour."

I ran my hand over it self-consciously. "Brown?"

"In the sunshine it looks red and blonde and brown. It's really pretty."

"Thank you." I tucked it behind my ears. So bad at the flirting thing.

"For Saturday, I'll pick you up at the Inn at eight, if that works for you."

"Sure." As I agreed, Trevor's truck pulled up into the parking lot with Murphy—his impressively muscular best friend—in the passenger seat. Murphy was the same age as Trevor, but he looked older because he was so massive and shaved his head bald. They both volunteered for Search and Rescue, and Murphy was training to be a paramedic. Trevor laughed at something Murphy said. Then they both eyeballed Steve in a cautionary way as he said goodbye to me and walked past the truck towards the school gym.

"Hey Deri," Trevor crooned in a mocking way as I slid in to the back seat.

"Hi. Hi Murph."

30

Murphy nodded his greeting and said, "Welcome home, Deri. Everyone missed you last year." He smacked Trevor's shoulder, then turned in his seat and studied my face with a perplexed expression.

"What?" I frowned and leaned back against the seat.

"You look different."

"Good different or bad different?"

"Well, that's kind of a trick question. It's not a bad different, but if I say it's a good different, you'll assume there was something wrong with how you looked before, which there wasn't. So. Just different. Right, Trev?"

Ignoring the good-versus-bad debate, Trevor lifted his chin in the direction Steve had gone and asked, "What was that?"

"What was what?" I mumbled.

"It looked like maybe you were getting asked out on a date."

Murphy seemed to enjoy the embarrassment that was probably evident from either the burning fuchsia cheeks, the sinking posture, or the slight groan. "We're just friends," I finally said to make them leave me alone.

"What's his name?" Trevor asked, as he shifted the truck into reverse and backed out of the parking stall.

"Steve."

"Steve what?"

"What difference does it make?" I shook my head and stared out the window, wishing he would drop it.

"I'm not going to let you go out with some random guy without doing a background check on him first."

"He's not random, and who made it your job to screen my boyfriends?"

"Oh, he's your boyfriend?" Trevor faked a gasp and shot an overly exaggerated incredulous look at Murphy.

"No, he's not my boyfriend, and I don't need you doing background checks on anyone. I'm not a little kid, and you're not my big brother."

31

"I'm still going to watch out for you. Nothing will stop me from doing that."

I glanced up and our eyes met in the rearview mirror. Based on how much his tone resembled the one he used when he was being protective over Kailyn, I knew he wasn't joking. I could take care of myself, but since my dad would have been comforted by Trevor keeping an eye on me, I didn't bother to argue.

Murphy broke the silence between us by telling me a story about how they got mugged at gun point in Brazil. Fortunately, they only had a small amount of cash on them and the guy didn't take their passports. Besides that incident, the rest of the stories sounded like amazing experiences.

Murphy was a member of the Squamish nation and his ancestors had lived in the Squamish area, literally, since the beginning of time. He was headed down to Britannia with us because Trevor's dad had planned a welcome-home barbecue for them with all the Search and Rescue volunteers. They never usually invited me to their parties, so when Murphy asked, "Are you coming?" my mouth dropped open in shock.

"Uh," I glanced at Trevor. His expression was completely indecipherable. "Trevor hadn't mentioned it, so I didn't know I was invited. But, I don't have any other plans tonight. So, I guess. Sure."

"Great," Murphy said, and punched Trevor's shoulder.

Trevor didn't appear impressed, and I wasn't sure if it was because he wished Murphy hadn't invited his honorary little sister to a party with every good-looking fire fighter, forest ranger, ski-patrol member, and pilot who lived in the Squamish district, or if the shot to the shoulder had actually hurt.

When we pulled into the parking lot in front of the Inn, the fire alarm was ringing. Trevor skidded to a stop as the guests crowded out the exits. Both he and Murphy jumped out before I even fully processed what was going on. Of all the worst-case scenarios for the Inn I'd been worried about, burning down was not one I had considered.

CHAPTER FIVE

Once I snapped out of my shocked stupor, I hopped out of Trevor's truck and wove through the flow of guests as they evacuated the Inn. I couldn't see or smell smoke, so I rushed into the lobby to search for my granddad. Murphy headed through the dining room towards the kitchen. Trevor took the stairs two at a time up to the second floor. I ran down the first-floor hall but stopped abruptly when I turned the corner and saw the problem.

Massive amounts of water poured from the ceiling through the light fixtures. It was already ankle deep. Not sure what to do, I stood stunned, motionless, and getting drenched until Trevor rushed down the hall and passed me. He leaned on the emergency-exit handle and pushed it outwards to let the water flow out into the parking lot. "Everything's fine upstairs," he said, not even out of breath. "But there is an elderly guest who needs help with the stairs. Ask your grandpa to turn the water off while I go back up and help her."

I nodded, but he was already gone before what he asked me to do sunk in. I sloshed through the water back towards the lobby. My granddad was out on the front porch and announced to the crowd, "It's just a false alarm. The fire department will assess the situation and give us the all clear to go back in shortly. Sorry for the inconvenience."

They mumbled things like how they should have stayed in a modern place in Squamish.

When Granddad saw me, his white caterpillar eyebrows angled together. "Why are you wet?"

"It's not a false alarm this time," I whispered and glanced at the unhappy guests. "The sprinklers are going off in the hall by my room. It's flooding."

"Did you see a fire?"

"No."

"Did you smell smoke?"

"No, and the sprinklers aren't going off anywhere else."

We both ducked back inside. He waddled around to check the panel behind the front desk, pushed his glasses up his nose, and squinted at the little lights. "It looks like a pipe burst." He turned and rushed towards the boiler room.

Ten seconds later, the screeching and clunking sounds of the water being shut off echoed through the building. The alarm stopped. Granddad appeared, grumbling about the rusted-out pipes and cursing the building for not being worth saving. He shook his head as he dialled the phone to call a plumbing company. I waded down the hallway towards my room, hoping the damage wasn't too bad.

It was bad.

Streams of water dripped out of the light fixtures, making them flicker. The floral wallpaper drooped over in heavy, sopping strips. The roof tiles were sagged in some areas, and broken in others. It looked horrible. Trevor and Murphy helped members of the volunteer fire department carry pieces of antique hallway furniture and my grandmother's oil paintings out to the parking lot. I quickly collected some of the more valuable items to help. It was already too late for the silk flower arrangements, which was fine. I never liked those dust collectors anyway. I arranged everything on a dry part of the parking lot and rushed back to find more things. Nothing else could be saved. When Trevor stepped inside, he ran his hands through his wet hair to push it off his face and smiled.

"Why are you happy?" I mumbled, fighting tears. "Everything's ruined."

"Don't worry. It can be fixed."

"We can't afford to fix it," I snapped, because if I didn't get angry, I was going to burst out in full-blown tears.

Knowing me as well as he did, he saw the panic underneath the frustration. "Insurance will cover it."

"Really?"

"Yeah. Cheer up." He mussed my hair and poked me in the ribs playfully. "You just got your renovations paid for."

I scanned the damage to the hallway, and a smile crept onto my face as I realized the disaster was potentially a great thing.

Trevor laughed as he reached up, removed the glass, shell-shaped covers to the wall sconces and tipped the water out of them. "When did you start wearing make-up? You look like that racoon we saved from drowning when we were kids."

"Gee. Thanks." I wiped my cheeks with the back of my hand, then swatted his arm. "What's wrong with wearing make-up?"

"Nothing." He turned his back to peel back a corner of wall-paper. "You don' need it, though."

Oh. Generally speaking, I was more interested in being respected for intelligence, and I didn't really buy into stereo-typical definitions of beauty, but it was a solid compliment coming from a guy who had high standards and only dated stunning women. My self-esteem didn't hinge on what others thought of me, but I had to admit it felt pretty good to know Trevor thought I was pretty when I was au naturel.

Murphy stepped in through the emergency exit with Trevor's dad, Jim, following him. Behind them was a line of Search and Rescue guys who had come down for the barbecue, but took a detour to help the fire department volunteers and check out the damage. Jim inspected the ceiling and wood floorboards, then asked the guys to help Trevor pull down strips of the soggy wallpaper.

"Did your room get wet?" Jim asked me.

Shit. I hadn't even thought to check. I didn't have a lot of stuff, and almost none of it was expensive. But a few of my dad's things were irreplaceable. I opened the door slowly and braced for the worst. To my complete relief it was perfectly dry, except for a little water that had seeped under the door seal.

Trevor smiled and winked in his I-told-you-everything-was-going-to-be-okay way. Jim and my granddad met at the end of the hall and discussed what should be done to prevent mold and to check the other pipes. When I heard the fire engines finally arrive outside, I stepped inside my room, closed the door behind me, removed my wet sweater, and hung it on the bathroom door to let it dry. My suede boots were ruined. My mom was going to be choked. I struggled to kick them off, then pushed the sopping skirt over my hips and down my thighs. I managed to inch it only as far as my knees when the door opened.

"Your grandpa wants you to—" Trevor stopped mid-sentence, still holding on to the doorknob. I froze mid-shimmy in an awkward semi-bent-over-knock-kneed stance. He stared at me for a second and grinned. I couldn't move. Eventually, he blinked and shook his head, as if he were trying to wake himself up. "Sorry. I was. I didn't know you were changing. Sorry. I should have knocked." He spun around until his back faced me. "Your grandpa wants you to do damage control with the guests. When you're finished changing."

He chuckled before he closed the door behind him. It was hard to tell if it was a *Ha ha, you look like such a dork* chuckle, an *Oh my God, I'm so embarrassed* chuckle, or a *Wow, Derian's not a little tomboyish girl anymore* chuckle. I glanced down at my worn baby-pink bra and plain white cotton Jockeys. Boring and mismatched. I groaned when I realized it was a *Ha ha, you look like such a dork* chuckle.

I flopped back on my bed and stared at the ceiling. As I lay there, a much bigger problem than the inadvertent peep show occurred to me. My granddad had asked me in July to mail the cheque to renew the insurance on the Inn. I couldn't remember doing it. I bolted up, panicked.

After I changed into dry clothes, I rushed to the front desk and rifled through the outgoing mail. The envelope wasn't there. I was relieved for a second until I remembered I had put it in my bag several weeks earlier to take it to the mailbox. I honestly couldn't remember actually dropping it into the mailbox, but it wasn't in my bag either. The company would have contacted us if it hadn't been received, right? I collected the mail every day and hadn't noticed any overdue notices. I bit at my fingernails, trying to visualize myself dropping it in the mailbox. I couldn't remember, so I tried to convince myself I must have mailed it because it wasn't in my bag, and they hadn't contacted us. The convincing wasn't working. My phone buzzed with a text from Sophie:

I heard Trevor and Murphy are having a Search and Rescue Party in Britannia tonight. You better get your ass next door and practice getting your flirt on.

Trevor saw me in my ginch. Too embarrassed to be anywhere near him.

I'm sure he was fine with the free show.

Doubt it. Old bra. Boy shorts. Soaking wet. Possibly see-through.

Wet? WTF?

Pipe burst. Inn flooded. Might have forgotten to renew the insurance for my GD. Can't remember mailing the cheque. Might be royally screwed. Long story.

CHAPTER SIX

I called the insurance company, but they wouldn't talk to me because my name wasn't on the policy. After a long, sleepless night, I broke down and told my granddad that I potentially screwed up badly. He called the adjustor in a panic. Fortunately, the company confirmed that the cheque had been received, so I relaxed about everything. Other than the fact that the corporate retreat booking asked for their money back, things seemed to be working out fine.

Trevor's dad lined up all the different trades to come in to do the repairs and renovations. Most of the plumbers, electricians, and framers were guys who volunteered for him at Search and Rescue. Only the plumbing had been worked on by the end of the week, though, because for the first four days, the industrial fans were set up day and night to dry out everything behind the plaster. I hadn't really slept much since it happened.

Since the guys all helped with the cleanup after the flood, the barbecue at Trevor's house had basically turned into a bunch of guys sitting around a bonfire drinking beer and eating hamburgers at midnight. I didn't go because I would have been the only female and I needed to be up early to make breakfast for the few remaining guests. On the bright side, the flood meant that the meeting with the real-estate agent had to be postponed, indefinitely.

On Saturday, after working a long shift at the front desk while my granddad ran errands, I got dressed in jeans and a white sleeveless top. Sophie had come over on Friday night to help me pick out the outfit and straighten my hair. She was definitely more excited about my pseudo-date with Steve than I was. Nervous was a better word to describe what I was.

At eight o'clock, I grabbed my purse and a cardigan and headed down the hall. The plywood sheets that acted as temporary floorboards bounced under each of my footsteps. When I pushed aside the plastic sheeting Jim had hung to keep the renovation dust contained to the first-floor hallway, I saw Trevor leaning his elbows on the lobby desk, dressed for the party in black jeans, a black T-shirt, and motorcycle boots. He smiled and stood up straight when I walked in. "Hey. Do you need a ride?"

"Uh, Steve is picking me up. Thanks anyway."

He narrowed his eyes, feigning a parental-type serious lecture face, which was obviously why he came by. "Steve Rawlings—the younger brother of Giselle Rawlings, third-string tennis player, and student council nerd—no offence."

I shot him an irritated glare to make it clear I wasn't in the mood for his ribbing, and he could spare me the impending lecture.

"You'll be happy to know I couldn't find any dirt on him. I tried, but he's squeaky clean."

"You didn't seriously ask around, did you?"

"Yeah, I did."

I shoved his shoulder as I walked past him. "You're not my brother. Stop acting like you are."

He seemed offended that I didn't appreciate his surveillance work and his tone changed. "I'm just making sure you're safe."

I stopped and spun around. "You're going to be at the party with us, remember? How much safer can I be?"

He smirked. "Well, unless you want me to tag along on all

your dates, he'd better be a nice guy who treats you right."

My own dad wouldn't have even been so nosey. Trevor was only two years older than me, and I didn't appreciate his attitude. With a snarky tone that I usually only reserved for my mom, I said, "Why don't you worry about your own life and leave me out of it? Thanks anyway." At first I felt guilty for being rude, but after he grinned at me in a self-satisfied way, I stormed out. Fortunately, Steve had already arrived in a white Ford Explorer. He hopped out and met me at the passenger-side door. I waited for him to open the door, but he didn't move.

He looked confused. "Doesn't your dad want to meet me first?"

"My dad's dead," I said, way too abruptly because I was still flustered by Trevor's meddling. Once I heard my own words, tears built up along my eyelashes. "Shit." I bit my lip to try to prevent the downpour.

Steve's face drained of all colour and his weight shifted as if he might fall down. "I'm so sorry, I can't believe I said that. I knew your dad was—I mean, I know that's why you were gone for a year. I blanked. I'm such an idiot. Sorry," he murmured. "Does your mom want to meet me?"

I grimaced and blinked slowly, which made the tears drip over the edge of my eyelashes. "My mom doesn't live with me. She's still in Vancouver."

Beads of sweat formed on his forehead. He pressed his lips together as if he didn't want to say anything else that might make things even worse. I turned my head to look back at Trevor. He was about five feet away and obviously heard the whole thing. As soon as he saw I was crying, he walked over, wrapped his arms around me, and pulled my head into his chest. His protectiveness made me cry harder. He hugged me for a while, then leaned his head down to whisper, "Your grandpa will want to meet your date. I'll go get him."

Trevor went back into the Inn and I wiped my palms across my cheeks. "Sorry," I sputtered.

"No, I'm sorry," Steve said quickly. "I don't know what I was thinking. I didn't mean to upset you."

The new Derian wasn't supposed to break down in tears every time someone mentioned her dad. First attempt didn't go that well.

My granddad rushed out the front door of the Inn and waved his arms around eagerly. "Here I am. Let's meet this young man who's taking Derian to a party."

I had to smile a little because my granddad looked cute with his white wispy hair flipping up on top of his head as he hustled to greet Steve. They shook hands and Steve answered a few questions. Trevor stood near the Inn door and gave me a look to see if I was okay. I mustered a smile and mouthed, *Thank you.*

I hugged my granddad and waved at Trevor, then got into the Explorer. Steve closed my door and jogged around the back to the driver's side. We didn't talk as we pulled out onto the highway and headed to Squamish. I could feel him glance over at me repeatedly. The reason I wasn't prepared for Steve to pick me up for a real date was because I tried to pretend it wasn't a real date. As far as I was concerned, we were going out as friends. I should have psyched myself and briefed my granddad to play the role of my absent parents.

"You look nice," he finally broke the silence.

"Thanks." I studied him with more attention. He had on jeans and a white dress shirt rolled at the sleeves. His blond hair was pushed back off his face in a different style than he wore at school. It suited him better. "I like your hair like that."

He blinked exaggeratedly, embarrassed. "My sister forced me to let her do it. I wouldn't normally admit to something like that, but she's going to be at the party and I can pretty much guarantee she's going to find a way to tell you that she styled it for me."

"It looks cute, but I'll tell her it doesn't if you want me to."

He smiled at my offer to back him up. "If you really do like it, I might wear it this way sometimes."

41

I inhaled deeply and rubbed my palms along my thighs. I tried to remind myself there was nothing to be nervous about. He was just my friend who I goofed around with at student council meetings. I grew up around Trevor and Murphy and I hung out with Doug and his friends all the time. A guy was a guy. A date didn't change that. Only, it kind of felt like it did.

"Are you okay?" He looked seriously concerned.

"I get a bit uncomfortable driving on the highway ever since my dad's accident. If you drive the speed limit I'll feel better."

"Oh. Sorry." He eased up on the accelerator and slowed down.

"Do you dance?" I asked to shift the conversation away from my anxieties.

"Uh, not well. Why? Is that a prerequisite?"

I shrugged because I didn't have a boyfriend prerequisite list, at least not that I knew of. "It's more fun to watch Sophie and the guys if you dance."

"Well, then we'll dance—or you'll dance and I'll try not to look like an idiot."

I laughed and relaxed a little for the rest of the drive. He was chatty, and there was no lull in the conversation once we were both feeling more comfortable. The party was at a huge house in Squamish to celebrate the nineteenth birthday of a girl who had gone to our school. Her name was Brandi. I didn't know her that well, but Steve's sister was her best friend. He'd known her most of his life.

The house was already packed with people when we arrived. The band hadn't started playing yet, so music cranked out of a stereo system. I spotted Sophie in the corner, setting up the extension cord for her mic. "I'll be right back." I squeezed Steve's hand, then walked over to Sophie and shouted in her ear, "Kill it!"

"You know it!" she yelled back. "How's it going with Steve?"

"Okay." I tucked my hair behind my ears.

"Uh-oh, only okay?"

"We got off to a rough start because he asked if my dad wanted to meet him."

She inserted the mic into the stand and adjusted the angle. "What a moron. Did you start bawling?"

"Yes."

"What did he do?"

"Nothing. Trevor was there, so he gave me a big hug and went to get my granddad."

Sophie's lips curled into a sympathetic pout. "Trevor is so sweet."

"He takes his big brother duties very seriously." I dropped my purse and cardigan next to the drums with Sophie's bag.

"Do something bold with Mason if you get the chance. You need to make a move."

"No. I'm not going to hit on a stranger. Even if I wanted to, I'd have no clue how to do that."

"Ask him to dance."

"I'm technically on a date with someone else, remember?"

She waved her hand dismissively. "Steve's just a pawn. Keep your eye on the prize."

Although chess was something I happened to be good at, I wasn't interested in being the type of person who played with people's feelings. I glanced around the party, feeling way out of my element. "I should probably get back to Steve before he thinks I ditched him."

"Don't forget you're on for the last song of the first set."

"No. Dirty Deri is not making an appearance tonight."

"Have a few drinks, she'll show up." She laughed and shoved my shoulder. "Go back to your date. It's not going to kill you to have some fun."

I exhaled and walked back across the room towards Steve. He was with his sister and Brandi. They laughed. He smiled uncomfortably as if they had just teased him a little.

"Happy birthday, Brandi," I said as I tucked in next to Steve.

"Thanks Derian. So you and Stevie, eh?" She pinched his cheek.

I didn't know if it was supposed to be a question or a statement, so I just smiled.

Steve cleared his throat and said, "Derian, this is my sister Giselle."

I sort of knew her from school. She used to be a cheerleader, but I had never formally met her before. I extended my hand to shake hers. "Nice to meet you."

"How do you like Stevie's new hairstyle?" She giggled as she held his chin and turned his head from side-to-side to show off her handiwork.

"I think it suits him."

"See! I told you," she shouted and shoved his chest, way too hyper.

"Okay," Steve said as he shooed her away. "See you later. Sayonara. Adios. Bu-bye."

Giselle and Brandi laughed at him, then wrapped their arms around each other and staggered away into the crowd as the band took their positions. Doug stepped up to the mic and Sophie sat down at the drums. She normally sang lead, but she played the drums for their opening number. Doug yelled in his deep, raspy punk voice, "Hit it!" The guys in the band stood in wide guitar stances with their heads hung and played in synchronization while Sophie pounded out the beat. The crowd went mental and slammed into each other in a mosh pit. Doug killed it and then passed the mic to Sophie for their second song, which was always Joan Jett because Sophie could make her voice sound awesomely raw like Joan's.

"Do you want to dance?" Steve asked.

"Sure, the next one they play is one of my favourites. It's a punked-out version of Joel Plaskett Emergency's old-school classic "Nowhere With You." Do you know it?"

"No, but if you can just jump around to it I should do all right."

Steve was a not bad dancer and, surprisingly, I was actually having a good time. We danced for at least five songs before taking a break, and I didn't even mind when he rested his hand on my waist as we walked off the dance floor.

"Do you want something to drink?" he shouted over the music.

Although Sophie suggested that a drink might help, I wasn't a drinker. I tried a sip of my dad's beer once, just to see what it was like. I didn't like it, at all. Plus, I preferred to have all my faculties at my disposal, so I said, "Water would be great. Thanks."

Steve nodded before he headed towards the kitchen, maybe slightly disappointed that I didn't want to get drunk. Or maybe he didn't care. I couldn't tell. I leaned my back against the wall and looked around. Trevor and Murphy were on the other side of the room surrounded by a group of girls. They were always surrounded by a group of girls, but as far as I could tell, Trevor wasn't dating anyone. He noticed me and tipped his glass. I waved at him, but then tucked my hair behind my ears and turned my focus towards the kitchen.

Steve held two bottles of water while he talked to Lisa Alvarez. She arched her back and flipped her long brown hair to flirt with him, the same way she acted with every member of the male species. I never understood why someone as pretty and smart as Lisa felt the need to be sleazy to get attention. I probably should have felt jealous, but I assumed she had a shitty home life or something, so I actually felt sorry for her. Steve chatted away with her, maybe oblivious to her tactics, or enjoying them.

Mason arrived through the front door, wove his way through the crowd, and leaned up against a wall by himself. I watched as he scanned the room. When his gaze reached mine, I froze. I wanted to look away, but for some reason I couldn't. I was stuck staring at him like a ditz. His expression didn't change, and he didn't look away either. I had never actually seen anyone as attractive as him, except in magazines and cologne commercials. If I didn't look away, he was absolutely going to think there was something stalkerish about me. Fortunately, Steve came back with the waters and blocked my view of Mason. "Are you having a good time?" He handed me one of the bottles.

"Yes." I chugged the entire thing. "Are you?"

"Definitely." He smiled and turned so he was beside me shoulder to shoulder. "You're a really good dancer."

"Thanks. I used to take lessons."

He smiled, and he was even cuter when he did. I hadn't noticed before. We talked for a while as Sophie sang old-school songs from The Killers, Green Day, and The White Stripes. Steve asked me to dance again. Then, when Sophie finished belting out "Bad Reputation", she called me on the mic, "Derian, get your scrawny ass up here."

"Shit," I mumbled as every set of eyes on the dance floor shifted in my direction. Sophie waved to coax me up on the stage. It was a toss-up which was more humiliating, let Dirty Deri loose or stand awkwardly in the middle of the room while everyone gawked at me. *The new Derian*, I reminded myself and took a deep breath. "Excuse me, Steve, that's my cue."

"Cue for what?"

I winked at him and said, "You'll see."

CHAPTER SEVEN

I reluctantly made my way through the crowd towards the stage, heart racing. The one and only time I had ever danced for the band had been less than a week after my dad's funeral. I was a distraught and angry wreck at the time, which apparently tapped into a latent punk side. Doug coined the term Dirty Deri when they were talking about my uncharacteristic flash dance the following day. I thought they were all making too big of a deal of it until I saw a video recording and shocked myself. I had to watch it twice before I believed it was me.

Without extreme grief to fuel me, I convinced myself it was just dancing and stood next to Sophie with my head hung, so my hair would fall forward to cover my face. Doug counted us in, and as soon as the guys started to play, I danced my very best punk rampage. Sophie cranked out the Ramones' "I Wanna Be Sedated." The crowd egged me on as I spun repeatedly and flipped my hair violently for effect. It was dizzying and invigorating at the same time. The lights blended into streaks and the music throbbed inside me like a heartbeat. For a minute, I forgot about the people watching me, my stress, everything, and just danced. I was free. Then it was over, and in time with the last drum beat, I flashed a two-handed devil horns and stuck out my tongue like a real rocker. It made the crowd cheer, although I was not even remotely badassed.

The band gave me high fives, then took a break. I walked back to Steve, not sure what he was going to think of my alter ego. He smiled, but it was kind of a dumbfounded smile. "That was awesome."

"Thanks. It's kind of stupid."

"No. It was cool. You must be thirsty again. I'll get you some more water." He rushed towards the kitchen.

I was sweating disgustingly, so I lifted my hair off the back of my neck to cool down. Hands slid across each side of my waist from behind. Air tickled my neck and Trevor's voice whispered, "Welcome back, Dirty Deri. Haven't seen you in a while."

His hands dropped away. I spun around to look at him, but he was already at least three strides away and headed out onto the deck. Not sure if it was his way of teasing or complimenting me, I turned back around. Mason Cartwright had crossed the room and was only a few feet away from me when Giselle bounded up and wrapped her arms around his neck. "Hey, new guy," she slurred. "You're sexy. Let's go hang out in Brandi's room. And by hang out I mean make out."

He ran his finger across his eyebrow, maybe uncomfortable by the proposition or the sloppy way she was hanging off him.

"Come on. I want to show you around." She stepped back and tugged his hand. He didn't budge. "Okay, I'll meet you upstairs. Don't take too long, though, because if I get bored, I might start without you."

Mason and I both stared at her because she didn't actually leave. She clutched her chest and wheezed, like she couldn't breathe. She winced as if a pain shot through her brain and then her eyes rolled back until only the whites showed. Before I had the chance to register what was going on, her body contorted and her legs collapsed. I lunged forward and tried to break her fall. I was too slow. Her head smashed against the stone fireplace

48

hearth with a horrific thud and her muscles clamped into a seizure.

"Giselle," I gasped as I knelt beside her. White foam bubbled out of the corners of her mouth. She continued to have a seizure. The blood from the back of her head pooled on the floor, turning her blonde hair red. Just like I'd seen in my vision. "Oh my God." I panicked. "Trevor! Trevor!" I screamed. He was already running towards me. He and Murphy were both at my side within seconds. As they knelt beside Giselle, I stood and stepped back, blood on my hands. I wanted to stop watching her convulsions, but I couldn't look away.

"Derian, call 911," Trevor ordered me.

I didn't have my phone. It was in my purse, which I'd left next to the drums with Sophie's. I was about to run and get it when I noticed Mason already talking on his phone. He gave me a look to indicate he was handling it. Steve pushed through the crowd and froze when he saw his sister seizing and bleeding all over the floor.

"Does she have any medical conditions?" Murphy asked Steve.

"No."

"Did she take anything?"

Distracted by her grotesque contortions, Steve didn't answer.

"Steve," Trevor said firmly, to snap him out of it. "Did she take any drugs?"

"I don't know. Maybe. I mean, she has before, so it's possible."

"Find out what she took and how much."

Steve turned and disappeared into the crowd. I couldn't watch anymore. Pushing between the people, I found the bathroom and used most of the liquid soap out of the dispenser to wash the blood off my hands. Even once they were clean, I didn't stop scrubbing. My stupid, useless visions. I hated them.

The ambulance siren got louder as it approached. Then it cut out when it stopped in front of the house. The red lights angled through the bathroom window and created hypnotic flashing patterns on the wall. At the very least, I could have prevented her fall if the warning had been more specific. Sick that it happened, I bent over the toilet and rested my hands on my knees for a while. Once the nauseous feeling passed, I sat on the edge of the bathtub and replayed the images of my dad's accident repeatedly in my mind. What was the point of seeing things ahead of time if I couldn't do anything to help the person? I beat myself up for not reacting quickly enough to break her fall until it occurred to me Steve was probably freaking out, and I was hiding in the bathroom like a wuss and a bad friend. After taking a few deep breaths, I forced myself to go back into the living room.

Giselle had stopped seizing and the paramedics strapped her to a stretcher. Steve looked horrible. I slid my hand around his. It trembled. "She's going to be okay," I whispered.

"I'm going to ride in the ambulance with her. Can you find a ride home?"

"Of course. Don't even worry about me. Just take care of your sister. I'll call you later."

The party kind of ended after the ambulance left. The band obviously didn't play their second set. The cops interviewed all Giselle's friends to find out more about the drugs she took. Brandi's parents showed up about half an hour later and everyone started to file out. Trevor walked over and wrapped me in a hug. "You okay?"

"No," I mumbled into his chest. "Is it all right if I get a ride home?"

"No, it's kind of out of my way." He chuckled and draped his arm across my shoulder to walk me out of the house.

"How can you be in the mood to joke?"

"I like emergencies. It's exciting, don't you think?"

"No. I don't think. I could have lived my entire life and been perfectly content without seeing someone overdose and crack their head open."

He opened the passenger side door of his truck for me. "But when you can help them, it feels good."

"I didn't help. Evidently, she was the girl I saw in my vision the other day, and even though I knew it was going to happen, I couldn't help her."

"It wasn't your fault. She's the one who took the drugs." He closed my door and walked around the hood to the driver's side.

After we'd been driving for a while, I asked, "Why do you think I see certain things and not others? And why do I see them at all if the clues don't make enough sense to prevent the accident?"

He frowned, giving it serious thought, but when he finally answered, he said, "I don't know. Maybe you should read that book I brought back from Peru for you. The woman said if you embrace your gift, you'll be able to develop it and use it with more deliberate skill."

"It's not a gift." I sighed and slouched in the seat. What Trevor didn't know was I had read up on intuition. A lot. After my dad died, I searched for answers. I wanted to know why I saw his accident in my mind with no details about who the driver was or when it happened. Without knowing it was my dad, there was no way for me to prevent him from driving down to see my mom that day. What was the point? No matter how much research on intuitive ability I did, the conclusions were always the same— everything happens for a reason, and we don't always know what that reason is. Not particularly helpful. Now another person was hurt, and I'd have to live with the visuals haunting me.

Trevor and I drove the rest of the way in silence and got home before I had a chance to calm down from the events of the night. With the images of Giselle contorted, bleeding, and foaming at the mouth still disturbing me, I wasn't looking forward to being all alone. After we parked, I asked, "Do you want to come in for popcorn and a movie?"

Even though watching movies together was something we used to do all the time when we were kids, we hadn't done it in at least five years. He took a long time to answer. "Which movie? I'm not going to sit through one of your cheesy eighties romance movies."

"How about *Lord of the Rings*?"

"No. Let's download a new release."

"The Wi-Fi isn't fast enough. It has to be one of my old classics."

He groaned, but reluctantly agreed.

I made the popcorn in the kitchen, grabbed a couple of bottles of juice, and joined him in my room. He had taken his jacket and boots off and sat widthways across my single bed, his back propped against the wall with pillows like a couch. He chose *Some Kind of Wonderful*, which was fine with me since it was one of my favourite eighties movies. I changed into pyjama bottoms in my bathroom, then sat next to him on the bed and set the bowl of popcorn between us.

I checked my phone to see if Steve had texted. He hadn't. I frowned and ate a couple of handfuls of popcorn.

Trevor mussed up my hair and said, "Don't worry. I'm sure she'll be fine."

"Do you really think so?"

He glanced at me and paused, hesitant to tell me what he really thought. "The doctors will take good care of her," was what he finally settled on. Then he took a handful of popcorn and pressed play on the movie to end the conversation.

When we finished the popcorn, I moved the bowl and slid down to rest my pillow on his thigh. Having him close reminded me of how empty my life had felt while I was gone. I had assumed all of the void was from not having my dad in my life anymore, but obviously some of the gaping hole was caused by not having Trevor to lean on either. "I missed you last year," I said quietly.

He ran his hand over my hair, which felt nice. Eventually, he said, "I missed you, too, Deri."

I fell asleep before the movie was over.

When I woke up in the morning, Trevor was gone and I was tucked under the covers. The book about intuition was on my bedside table. Before I made breakfast for the guests, I texted Steve to see how Giselle was doing. At about eight o'clock, he wrote back: *Not good.*

CHAPTER EIGHT

Steve missed two weeks of school. His sister was put in a medically induced coma to reduce the swelling on her brain and allow time for her organs to recover from the damage of the Fentanyl-laced cocktail of synthetic party drugs she had taken.

Even once Steve came back to class, he was a zombie, and he left right after school every day to visit her in the hospital. I checked in with him to see how she was doing. But he didn't want to talk about it, so I gave him his space.

Trevor picked up more hours at the dock and couldn't give me a ride after school anymore. The bus that went to Britannia Beach in the afternoon left every ninety minutes. If I missed the one right after school, I had to find something to do to burn time. One afternoon in October, I stayed late in the art room to work on some sketches for my architecture portfolio. When I left, I assumed the halls would be empty. I was completely startled when I turned the corner by my locker and interrupted Mason Cartwright making out with Lisa Alvarez. They were going at it pretty good. His right arm was elbow deep up the front of her shirt, while her hand moved across the front of his jeans in a very purposeful way.

"Uh, sorry. Excuse me. Sorry," I scrambled awkwardly, pointing at my locker, which he was leaned up against.

Mason stepped to the side and extended his arm straight forward to keep Lisa at a distance.

I glanced at him for half a second. "I just have to get my coat. Sorry." I covered the side of my face with the palm of my hand so I couldn't see them as I rushed to collect my stuff. Because I was flustered and only using one hand, I dropped my books. The sketches slid across the floor. Mason bent to pick them up for me. I stuffed everything in my locker randomly, but then the door wouldn't close. I had to jam it violently until I could cram the lock back on. Completely mortified, I turned and jogged down the hall away from them.

The bus was going to be another ten minutes, so I sat on the bench and pulled out a history textbook to read. My head was down when a truck pulled up in front of me. It was the 4Runner. Trevor leaned across the cab and opened the passenger side door from the inside with his trademark grin. "Do you need to help out at the Inn?"

"No. Not today. There are only two guests."

"Murphy and some of the guys are going to Rusty's to grab something to eat. You'll be the only girl and you'll be the only one who doesn't need a shower. Do you want to come?"

Sit and wait for the bus by myself as the sky threatened rain, or hang out at a pub with a bunch of rowdy guys. "Sure. Isn't it every girl's dream to be one of the guys?"

He laughed. "I don't know what girls dream about."

I hopped in. He pulled back out on the road, then turned the corner to head to Rusty's.

"Call your grandpa and tell him where you are."

"Wow. You're worse than my mother." I shook my head to mock him and pulled out my phone. After I hung up, I joked, "He said I'm not supposed to take rides from strangers."

"Good thing I've known you most of your life." He glanced at me and grinned. "Do you remember the first day we met?"

"Yeah, you had your red hat on backwards and you hopped

out of the moving truck, holding your baseball mitt like you owned the place. You haven't changed that much—just taller."

"I was bummed when I saw you sitting on the deck of the Inn playing Barbies."

"Bummed? Why?"

"I was hoping to move next door to a really cool boy who would want to do things like play baseball, catch frogs, and build tree forts with me."

"I did all those things with you."

"I know, but—" We parked at the restaurant and continued to talk as we walked across the parking lot. "When I first saw your long, shiny hair and girly, pink clothes, I thought you'd be prissy." He held the restaurant door open for me. "What did you think of me when we first met?"

"I saw a cocky looking athletic kid with a smirky smile and I thought, there's the boy I'm going to marry when I grow up."

His eyebrows shot up and his smile transitioned into surprise.

Air caught in my throat when I realized what I'd actually said. *Why did I blurt that out? So embarrassing.* My heart seized as I scooted past him through the doorway into the waiting area. Two girls who had graduated in his year were just leaving but stopped to say hi to him and touch his arm unnecessarily frequently. He told one of them he would call her later and they left. The hostess wasn't at her station, but fortunately I could see on the far side of the restaurant that Murphy was already at a table with his equally muscular older brother and two other guys from Search and Rescue. I made a beeline for them. I didn't even check whether Trevor was trailing, laughing at me.

The guys moved over in the booth and made room for us to squeeze in. Trevor was right behind me, which was confirmed when he placed his hand on my waist and let me slide in first. Wedged between him and Murphy, I still refused to look at him. If I had believed, at any point in the eleven years I had known him, that we were in the same league, I would have developed a giant crush on him. Since we were so obviously not even playing in the same sport, let alone same league, I let go my childhood fantasy of marrying him before I even hit puberty. Well, I thought I had let it go, until it shot out of my mouth just to humiliate me.

"So, you think you can hang with the big boys, eh?" Murphy nudged me.

I shrugged, not convinced I could.

"You already know my brother Ryan, and this is Colton and Bobby."

"Hi." I smiled at all of them, glad to be included in their boys' time. Although, to be honest, it was pretty stinky. I finally looked at Trevor's face, prepared for him to tease me about the marriage comment. To my total relief he smiled—looking relaxed.

"How many chicken wings can you eat, Deri?" Murphy asked.

"Maybe five."

They all laughed. "Be prepared to be disgusted," Trevor said.

The waitress brought out two huge platters full of wings and placed them in front of Murphy and Ryan. "First one to finish doesn't have to pay," Murphy explained.

I frowned at the heaping portion. "How many chickens had to die for this?"

"Their deaths weren't in vain. We're going to thoroughly enjoy their sacrifice." Murphy chuckled, then pretended to be serious, "Do you want me to do a little prayer of gratitude first?"

"I think you should do a prayer that you don't choke and die," I quipped.

"No worries. Trevor knows the Heimlich."

"Go!" Murphy's brother yelled and they dug in.

Trevor smiled at me apologetically. "I warned you."

Yes, he did warn me. I came of my own free will. By the time I finished my salmon burger and all my yam fries, they were still working on the platters of wings. The bones were piled up on a third plate like a chicken graveyard. Murphy won by three wings.

"Okay, Deri, how much money do you have on you?" he asked.

"Um, like twenty bucks."

"I bet you twenty bucks I can eat one of every dessert on the menu."

"That's all the money I have. I won't be able to pay for my burger."

He waved his hand to dismiss my concern. "Trevor can cover your meal."

I smiled because, although Trevor hadn't intended for it to be a real date, the thought of him paying for my meal made it seem like one.

"Twenty bucks if I eat one of every dessert on the menu," Murphy repeated.

I read the menu closely. There was no way he could eat all eight dessert choices after the platter of wings he'd ingested. I was just about to take his bet when Trevor subtly shook his head side to side.

"Stay out of it, Maverty," Murphy warned.

Trusting Trevor's subtle caution, I leaned my elbows on the table and stared Murphy down. "How about you give me one hundred dollars if I can eat one of every dessert on the menu," I counter-challenged.

"Interesting." He sat back and stroked his chin exaggeratedly as he considered it. "What do I get when you can't do it?"

"I will clean your and Ryan's house until it no longer smells like a gym locker."

The guys all cheered. Murphy enthusiastically swung his tree trunk arm in the air to get the waitress' attention. She walked over and pulled out her little writing pad. "What can I get for you, Murph?"

"One of every dessert for the girl."

"For the girl? What's the bet?"

"A hundred dollars if she can do it, and she cleans our house when she can't."

"Gross." The waitress wrinkled her nose. "I'll be right back."

"You mean *if* I can't, not when," I corrected him.

"No, I mean when."

The waitress returned a few minutes later with two other servers. They arranged the eight plates in front of me.

"Hey!" Murphy protested. "Those are small portions."

The waitress smiled and shrugged innocently. Even with the smaller portions, I didn't think I could do it. "Good luck," she said and pointed across the room. "The bathrooms are over there if you need."

I started with the ice cream, so it wouldn't melt. Then worked my way through a fluffy strawberry cheesecake, a chocolate mousse, Jell-O, pumpkin pie, and apple crumble. The first six actually went down not too badly, but I had a pecan tart and a chocolate-caramel pound cake left. "I made an error," I moaned. "I should have gone from dense to fluffy." I rested my cheek on the table.

"You can do it, Deri," Trevor encouraged me. "Think about how bad their rooms are going to smell. They'll probably make it extra rank just for you."

I sat up and aimed a forkful of pecan tart into my mouth. Fortunately, the slice wasn't that big and I finished it in four bites. I had to rest my head back on the table. Murphy's brother laughed at me. "I'm going to leave my sweaty gym clothes rolled up in a ball in the corner for a week and let food go rotten in the fridge before you come over."

I moaned.

"I'm going to leave dirty dishes in the sink and let meat and fish garbage pile up." Murphy laughed. "Maybe there will be maggots."

"No. Stop talking. I can do it. I just need some liquid."

Trevor handed me a glass of water, then rubbed my shoulders as if I were a boxer about to go another round. "You can do it. One more and then you can puke if you have to."

The other guys chanted, "Deri, Deri, Deri."

The food I had already eaten threatened to come back up. I drank one more sip of water and took a deep breath. The sugar rush surged, but I shovelled the pound cake down in six forkfuls. My throat struggled to swallow the last bite, but I choked it back and said, "I did it."

"Let's see," Murphy made me open my mouth to prove I actually swallowed.

They all cheered and pounded the table. I got dizzy and then my stomach churned. "Move, move, move." I slapped Trevor's shoulder in a panic.

He slid out of the booth and I ran to the bathroom. They all laughed behind me. I burst into a stall and puked out every one of the eight desserts. Then the salmon burger and the yam fries. Cleaning their house probably would have been less disgusting. I stood over the toilet for a long time, waiting to see if I was going to get sick again.

"You okay, honey?" I flushed the toilet and opened the cubicle door. It was the waitress, smiling at me. "Trevor sent me in to make sure you're okay."

"I'm fine. I did it."

"I heard. Good job. Murphy is the only other person who's ever done that. Trevor tried once and puked after four."

"Really?" I asked as I washed my hands and rinsed my mouth out with water.

"Here." She handed me a piece of gum. "I'm impressed you held your own."

"Thanks for the small portions."

She winked and went back into the restaurant. I splashed water on my face, also impressed that I held my own. Sophie would have been proud. When I joined the guys back at the table, Murphy handed me five twenty-dollar bills. "There you go. Good job."

"I heard you puked after four," I teased Trevor and needled my elbow against his ribs.

"She gave me huge portions," he yelled, so the waitress could hear.

He stretched his arm along the back of the booth behind me, and we had so much fun laughing about other stupid bets Murphy had done. Hanging out with boys was my comfort zone. Too bad a proper date was a different story. It was almost nine o'clock when Trevor and I got back to Britannia.

"Thanks," I said after we got out of the truck. "I had a really good time."

He nodded to agree. "I guess their house is going to stay rank. What are you going to spend the money on?"

I shrugged because I hadn't actually given it any thought. "I'll probably still hire a cleaning service for them."

"You don't have to do that. Keep the money and splurge on something you wouldn't normally buy for yourself."

I tried to come up with something I would want to buy with a hundred bucks. After a long pause, I still couldn't think of anything. "There's nothing I really want."

"A girl who doesn't like to shop? Weird. I guess you're officially one of the guys now. Murphy's going to challenge you to a wing race next time, so be prepared."

"I can take him," I joked, secretly glad he implied a next time.

He spun his keys around his thumb before he shot me the same smirky smile from the day he moved to Britannia Beach. "So, you want to marry me some day, huh?"

Damn. I hoped he'd forgotten about that. I dropped my head so my hair fell forward and hid the blush in my cheeks. "I was five. I didn't even know what I was thinking."

"Sure." He reached over and mussed up my hair as if I were a little kid.

"Seriously?" I protested and pushed his hand off my head.

He laughed and turned to walk away. "Night," he called over his shoulder.

I sighed. "Night."

I watched as he turned and walked up his porch steps. Eventually, I went into the Inn. Being one of the guys didn't actually feel much more mature than being his little sister, but at least it was something different.

My granddad was behind the front desk, his head rested in his hands in a depressed way. A letter lay on the desk next to his elbow.

"What's wrong?"

He glanced up at me and took a deep breath before he answered. "The insurance company rejected the claim for the flood."

"What?" A million scenarios for what that would mean raced through my head simultaneously. None of them were good. As my mouth dropped open, I mumbled, "Shit."

CHAPTER NINE

I texted Doug as soon as I found out the insurance claim had been rejected. I asked him to meet me in the courtyard after school. He didn't even ask why. He just agreed.

"What's up?" He sat on the table part of the picnic table next to me.

Desperate to fix things so my granddad wouldn't need to come up with enough money to pay for all the renovations out of pocket, I had thought up a plan. Doug had the skills needed to help me with it. The only problem was it could potentially get us both sent to Juvie. "Would you do something illegal for me?"

"Probably."

"Okay. Thanks." I stood because I already changed my mind about getting him involved.

"Is that it?"

I bit at my bottom lip, weighing my options. "I don't want to talk about it here. Can you go for a drive?"

"Sure. Sophie has choir until four-thirty. I have to be back in time to pick her up."

"It won't take that long. I'll explain what I need you to do. You can decide whether you want to be a part of it or not."

He frowned, both concerned and intrigued at the same time.

"Sophie would be so mad at me for asking you to do something that might breach your probation. Promise you won't tell her"

"Yeah. Whatever."

"Promise not to tell her."

"I promise. Geez, what's gotten into you?"

"Let's just go." I walked with him to his car, feeling frazzled, and determined, and guilty, and terrified. Doug drove an old black Chevy Nova. It was so loud it set off alarms when it passed by parked cars. A little difficult to be inconspicuous in it.

"Where are we going?" he asked.

"It doesn't matter as long as it's private. How about the old railroad station?"

He peeled out onto the street in front of our school. But then drove the speed limit once we were on the highway. He knew it bothered me to drive fast. "What is it you want me to do, exactly?"

"Hack into the computer system of an insurance company and change the file to say the claim was approved."

"Is this about the flood at the Inn?"

I nodded, wishing I wasn't desperate enough to get a friend in trouble. But I was, if he was willing. "What would happen to your probation if you got caught doing something illegal?"

"I'd probably have to do a couple months in Juvie. But I wouldn't get caught."

"So, you think you can do it?"

His mouth angled as if I'd insulted him. "Child's play." About ten minutes later, he pulled into the dirt parking lot in front of the abandoned railroad station where the band sometimes partied. He leaned into the back seat and pulled his laptop out of his bag. I watched as he inserted some sort of gadget stick into the USB port and turned the computer on. It was interesting to watch him work. He typed really quickly, navigating through a bunch of script pages that looked like hieroglyphics to me. When he asked for it, I handed him a copy of the previous year's policy. Within minutes, he stopped typing and read for a while. "The claim says it's approved."

"Really? It was that easy to change it?"

He glanced at me and raised his eyebrow. "FYI, what I just did was not easy, but that's not what I meant. I mean, their records show it being approved. Why do you think it was denied?"

"We got a letter from the company." I dug it out of my bag and handed it to him.

He pushed his glasses up and scrolled down on the computer screen to read more. "It must be a mistake. The claim was approved and sent to some guy named Len Waddell for processing. He must have sent the wrong letter. It should be easy to clear up if your grandpa talks to the company."

"Really? That's great. Can you make it so they won't know we were messing around with it?"

He tilted his head and grinned at me. "I can make it rain out here."

I looked over my shoulder and scanned the empty grass lot. "I believe you."

He laughed and typed until the screen went blank.

CHAPTER TEN

Without actually admitting how I knew for sure a mistake had been made, I was able to convince my granddad it would be a good idea to request the insurance company double check the records. It wasn't difficult to persuade him. Like Trevor, my granddad trusted my intuitions without asking too many questions. The insurance company representative told him the review process could take weeks, so there was nothing else to do but keep paying on credit and wait.

The next day at school, I checked in with Steve at his locker. His sister was still in a coma, stable but critical. Ever since it had happened, I had tried each night to conjure up some sort of vision about her recovery, but nothing came to me. So much for practicing to get better at it. Steve didn't like talking about Giselle that much, so I tried to come up with other things to ask him. "Did you start the assignment for Mrs. Tookey's class?"

"No. I haven't been able to focus on homework."

"I'll help you catch up if you want. We can meet in the library after school."

He shook his head, and it seemed to take all his energy to do it. "Thanks. I can't today. Maybe another day."

I sighed and watched him stuff his bag into his locker. Right before the bell, Sophie walked by us. I called her name, but she kept walking as if she hadn't heard me. "I'll see you later, Steve. Let me know when you want to meet to do homework." I ran after Sophie. She walked fast, books clutched to her chest. "Soph!" She turned the corner and kicked open the bathroom door with the sole of her knee-high Dayton's. I followed her in. "What's wrong?"

She slammed her books down on the shelf above the sinks and glared at me. A grade-eight girl walked into the bathroom and Sophie snapped, "Get out!" The girl turned and ran back out into the hallway. "What did you do yesterday after school?"

My mouth went dry. "Uh. I went to the art room for a while, then I hung out at the library until it was time to catch the bus."

"Really?"

I twirled a strand of my hair so tightly it cut off the circulation to the tip of my finger. Hanging out with Doug without her wasn't something I needed to lie about, but I was reluctant to be honest since she'd flip if he got arrested because of me. "Why?"

"Lisa Alvarez told me she saw you and Doug take off in his car. Is that true?"

Busted. I exhaled slowly. "Yes, but—"

She shook her head in a disappointed way, then picked up her books and bumped her shoulder into mine as she walked past me.

I spun around. "Sophie. I'm sorry. I didn't tell you because—"

She waved her arm over her head and kept walking. "Save it. I don't have time for liars."

Sophie completely blew me off for the rest of the day. Normally, she was cool about things, and even when she was mad, the cold shoulder usually only lasted for a few hours before she was over it. For some bizarre reason she was still super-pissed after school. She wouldn't even look at me when I walked over to her locker and said, "Hi."

The next day, I assumed she would be over it since it wasn't that big of a deal, and we didn't technically do anything that would get Doug in trouble. To my complete shock, when I walked up to our regular lunch table, she glared at me and said, "Go away, liar."

It felt as if she kicked me in the kidney. My eyes watered and Doug shrugged in an apologetic way. I walked away before I started bawling and sat on the floor at my locker to eat my lunch by myself. Sophie had a mean streak when it came to fake or judgmental people, and I had witnessed her hostility for years, but it had never been directed at me before. It was such an uncharacteristic overreaction, which left me equally hurt, remorseful, and confused.

Mason Cartwright and a girl named Izzy turned the corner, holding hands. I wiped my eyes with my sleeve so they wouldn't see I was crying. Izzy yammered on about something that sounded gossipy and didn't notice me. He did. He looked down at me and hesitated, concerned I was upset. She tugged at his hand. I averted my eyes to send the signal that I didn't want him to ask what was wrong. He reluctantly kept going.

Nikolai walked up and smiled as if he knew exactly how I felt. "Do you want to eat lunch together?"

He was such a sweetie. I took a deep breath and blinked to lessen the sting of the tears. "I would love that." I patted the ground next to me. "Have a seat."

He sat crossed-legged and opened his brown paper lunch bag. He pulled out a sandwich, bit into it, chewed for a while, and then pushed his glasses up on his nose. "Why were you crying?"

Not wanting to bore him with my problems, I shrugged and said, "I'm having a bad day. How's it going with you?"

"Good, but I suck at French. Why aren't you hanging out with your cool friends?"

I shoved his shoulder playfully. "I am."

He looked perplexed for a second. Then he realized I was

referring to him. "Ha ha. Good one. I'm the opposite of cool."

"Obviously not. You're having lunch with a grade-eleven girl. That's pretty cool for a grade-eight boy."

"Do you mind if I tell my friends we kissed?"

I laughed at the irony since it would be the only kissing gossip I had ever been included in. "I guess that would be all right. I wouldn't want you to lie, though." I leaned over and kissed his cheek. "There you go. Now it's true."

He grinned and his face turned red. "Thanks."

"No. Thank you. I was feeling really sad. You made me feel better."

"Any time."

Steve wandered over with his hands shoved in his pockets. He looked back and forth between Nikolai and me. "Hey."

"Hi. Do you want to join us?" I asked.

He slid his back down a locker and sat on the floor beside me. "How's your sister doing?"

"A little bit better. They brought her out of the coma. Her liver is still not functioning properly on its own, though."

I shared my grapes with him because he didn't have a lunch. "How are you doing?"

He shrugged, as if he wasn't even sure. "I'm going to start playing tennis again." He glanced at Nikolai, then asked me, "Would you like to go for coffee some time? Just friends."

I nodded and smiled. "Sure."

The following day, Trevor came by the Inn for breakfast. He filled a plate at the buffet table. I served him his coffee with cream, no sugar. Once it was less busy, I sat down at table across from him.

"Morning, sunshine," he said as he flicked a straw wrapper at my arm. "How's it going?"

"Not great," I mumbled and slouched.

"Why?"

"Lots of reasons." I fidgeted with the fork.

69

"Sophie's still mad at you?"

I glanced up at his face. "Yeah. I didn't know you knew about that."

"Doug mentioned you guys were fighting."

"Did he mention what her problem is? She's being completely unreasonable. It's so unlike her to unleash her fury on me, especially for something that really wasn't that big of a deal. I don't know what to do."

He shrugged and split one of my famous apple-cinnamon muffins. He gave half to me and took a bite of the other half. "What did you lie to her about?"

"Nothing. It was so stupid. She asked me if I had been with Doug the other day after school. I told her I hadn't because he and I had agreed not to tell her. She found out anyway."

Trevor frowned and studied my face. "Why did you have to lie about being with Doug? Is something going on between you two?"

"No." I looked over my shoulder to check if anyone could overhear us. "It's nothing like that. I asked him to hack something for me, and I didn't want anyone to know because he's on probation for that vandalism thing. I should have just told her the truth. Ironically, she wouldn't have cared about the illegal hacking part, but the lying part is like a mortal sin. It's just so weird that she's still mad."

Trevor's shoulders relaxed and he leaned back to peel an orange. "It's not about you. Doug sort of hinted that Sophie is going through some shit and she's not coping that well."

"What kind of shit? I've been her friend since kindergarten. Why wouldn't she tell me if she had a problem?"

"I don't know, Deri. You need to talk to her."

"I tried. She won't return my messages."

"Well, maybe you just need to be patient. Everyone was pretty patient with you while you went through everything you went through last year."

I nodded, remembering how unconditionally supportive

Sophie had been after my dad died. And how when we were growing up, she always stood up for me. "I miss her."

"Don't worry too much about it. She's not going to throw away your entire friendship over one mistake." He separated the orange segments and offered me one.

"Oh my God, Trevor. What happened to your hand?"

He rotated his wrist to look at the gouged knuckles on his right hand. "A guy fell over the falls. While we hoisted the basket up the cliff face, the balance shifted, smashing my hand against the rock. It doesn't hurt. This does, though." He stretched his leg out from under the table to show me the stitches that ran down his shin. "I slipped and a jagged edge stabbed me. Every time I move, it kills."

I reached across the table to steal another segment of orange from him. "Remind me why you voluntarily risk your life for strangers."

He laughed. "It's fun."

When we were younger, I used to always get a sick feeling before Trevor got hurt. It was never actually a vision, more of a dread. It hadn't happened in a couple years, though, which was maybe a sign that my brain glitch was going to continue to fade as I got older. Or, maybe I didn't feel it anymore because we weren't as close as we used to be as kids. I wasn't sure how I felt about that.

"How's it going with Steve Rawlings?" he asked.

"We're just friends." I picked up a spoon and stirred my cold tea. "He's dealing with a lot of stress still."

He took a sip of his coffee and folded a paper napkin into tiny creases with his left hand. "What are you doing on Saturday night?"

"Um. Nothing. Why?"

"A guy at work was giving away two tickets for the stage musical of *Footloose* in Vancouver. His wife can't go because she has to work. I thought you might be interested since you're into eighties crap. Do you want to go?"

Oh my God, what? Like a date? Did Trevor Maverty just ask me out? I lost motor function and dropped the spoon on the table. *No. Why would he mean a real date? Don't be stupid. I think he did.* I tried a couple times to open my mouth to answer. On the third try, words came out. "Sure. That sounds fun. Thank you." I had to dig my fingers into my knees to prevent my legs from bouncing around. "What time should I be ready?"

"Around five and we'll go for dinner downtown first. I can drop you off at your mom's apartment after the show if you want to spend the night there."

Holy cow. That sounds like a real date. Motor function returned and I almost shot up from my chair to do some cheerleader leaps. "You can stay over with me," I blurted out, then realized how forward it sounded. "I mean, in the guest room."

"Sure. If your mom's okay with it." He stood and picked up his dirty plate. "So, I'll see you on Saturday."

I nodded like a springy dashboard doll.

"I'll let myself out the kitchen exit." He smiled and walked towards the kitchen with his plate.

A sweet, smart, outdoorsy, good-looking guy like Trevor was exactly who I always imagined myself ending up with at some point. It never occurred to me it would happen so soon, nor that it could literally be Trevor. I reminded myself he hadn't called it a date, but then I decided it didn't matter because if we had an awesome time, it could maybe lead to a real date. After letting the enormity of what just happened sink in, I ran into the lobby and released my happy dance, which was a mixture of the running man, a hand jive, and a Beyoncé booty bounce.

"Did you win the lottery?" My granddad laughed.

"I'm definitely feeling lucky."

"Me too." He smiled and handed me a letter. "I got an offer on the Inn from a developer."

I abruptly stopped jigging around.

CHAPTER ELEVEN

On Saturday, I woke up early. Insane butterflies ricocheted around in my stomach due to my unclearly defined outing with Trevor. I also had severe muscle tension through my shoulders due to the unclearly defined sale of the Inn. To shake off the jitters, I went for a trail run. The smell of giant cedars and Douglas firs filled my lungs. The sun dappled through the boughs and the silence was so serene, but it didn't help with my nerves. When I thought about the possibility that Trevor might like me as more than a friend, a tickling sensation danced all over my skin. When I thought about the offer on the Inn, a jabbing sensation cut through my brain like tiny little daggers.

I still had the whole day to get through, so after my run I kept my excitement and panic at bay by doing inventory and placing the orders for cleaning supplies we needed. While I had Windex on my mind, I proceeded to wash the windows in the dining room, lobby, and library. They were heritage frames with eight glass panels each, and there were ten across the front of the Inn, so it took a while. It wasn't intellectually challenging enough to keep me distracted from watching the clock, though, so I dove into some bookkeeping. Unfortunately, since we hadn't been that busy, I completed the accounts payable in fifteen minutes. It was only noon. I glanced over at Trevor's house, wondering if he was excited too. Lucky for him, they got called out on a rescue while I was on my run, so at least he was busy with something interesting. I sat at the computer and opened up the Inn's website administration page to make some random updates it didn't need. How did people who dated all the time do it?

Around three o'clock, I desperately wanted to call Sophie and ask her what I should wear. I held my phone in my hand and stared at it for a long time. Normally, planning my date outfit would have been something she would have killed for—especially for what could arguably be considered a first date with Trevor. Eventually, I called, but she didn't answer.

Without her help, I felt completely lost. After a lot of deliberation, I decided to wear a black dress that I'd worn at a New Year's party the year before. It was fitted and draped over only one shoulder in a borderline sexy way, but still classy. I straightened my hair and painted my nails red. Pink maybe would have been a better choice, but it was too late to change them.

My mom was thrilled we were staying over, and she already had the menu planned for Sunday brunch. Not that Trevor would probably see what I was going to wear to sleep in, but I packed my cutest pyjama shorts and a tight spaghetti-strap tank top just in case.

At four-thirty, my phone rang. It was Sophie. She was crying. Sophie never cried. "Deri, I need you. Can you come over?"

"What's wrong?"

"My parents had a huge blow out. My dad packed all his things. He left, and he's not coming back."

Sophie's parents were the mildest-mannered people I had ever met. I couldn't even imagine them fighting, let alone breaking up. "I'm sure it's temporary. They'll work it out. They just need time to calm down."

"My mom wants a divorce. She told him not to come back."

Normally, nothing fazed Sophie, so it crushed me to hear her break down. Part of me always knew that being tough was her defence mechanism, but proof that she wasn't completely invincible scared me a little. She had always been a protector, a confidence-builder, and the best best friend I could have ever asked for. I wasn't exactly sure how to be there for her the way she had always been there for me, but I knew I owed her. She needed me immediately and it wasn't something that could be rescheduled. Trevor and I could always go out some other night. Hopefully.

"I'll be there as soon as I can." I hung up and ran over to Trevor's house. I knocked loudly, waited two seconds and knocked again. I peeked through the glass inset in the door and saw him coming down the stairs wearing dark-grey dress pants and no shirt. His toothbrush hung out of the corner of his mouth as he opened the door.

"Hey. You're early." He motioned with his arm to invite me in. "You look nice."

"Thanks." I stepped in and tried not to stare at his bare chest. He smelled amazing. Why? Why did he have to smell so amazing? I didn't want to cancel, but I had to. It would have been selfish not to.

"So, you can't wait to get *Footloose*?" he joked.

"I. It's. Um, yeah." I couldn't speak properly because he looked incredibly hot. Not that he hadn't always been hot, but looking at him as someone who might actually want to date me made everything appear different. "I. You look nice, too, by the way. Or, half of you looks nice. The half that's dressed up. The other half looks good too. Sorry. What was I saying? Oh, yeah. I was really looking forward to tonight."

He seemed amused by my weirdness. "Was?"

"Something important has come up. I really don't want to, but I have to bail. I'm so sorry." Really, really sorry. Devastated actually.

"Is everything all right?"

"Well, with me, yes. With Sophie, no. She called me, crying."

"Sophie was crying?"

"I know, right. I couldn't believe it. I'm not sure if I was more shocked that she called, or that she was crying."

"What happened?"

"Her parents had a big fight. Her dad moved out. I have to go to her."

"Yeah. Of course. I understand."

Of course he understood. He was an awesome person. That only made it harder to pass up my chance to go out with him. Hopefully there would be another opportunity. I leaned in and kissed his cheek. "Thanks for being so sweet."

He smiled in an almost shy way and ran his hand through his hair.

"I really am sorry. I'll pay you back for the tickets."

"I got them for free, remember? Maybe Murphy can use them." He balanced his toothbrush back into the corner of his mouth and talked around it. "Let me finish getting dressed. I'll give you a ride to Squamish." He turned to go back up the stairs. I watched his ass until he turned the corner. *Oh my God, I just watched Trevor's ass in an I-wouldn't-mind-touching-that-ass way.* What was going on in the universe?

To distract myself from the very surreal idea of Trevor and me being a couple, I called my mom and told her we weren't coming. She sounded nearly as disappointed as I felt. For the first few months after I moved back to Britannia, I really didn't have any desire to see her, but more recently I had started to miss her. I promised to come down soon and hung up with a heavy feeling inside. In the living room, Kailyn leaned over the coffee table, flipping through an old telephone book. She rocked which she only did when she was upset.

"Hey, Kiki. What are you looking for?"

"My mom's phone number."

"Oh." I glanced into the kitchen to see if Jim had heard. He was distracted. It smelled as if he had burned something on the stove. "That phone book is only for Squamish. I don't think she lives around here. Her number won't be in there."

She kept searching as if she didn't hear me. She ran her finger down the page and her lips moved as she read the names.

"Why do you want to call her?"

"I need to talk to her about girl stuff. I live with boys who don't know anything."

"I'm a girl. You can ask me whatever you want."

"You're too little."

I didn't think I was too young to be of any use, but arguably I was too inexperienced, depending what she needed help with. "How about my mom? She won't mind if you call her. Or, if you want, Trevor and I can take you down to Vancouver one day to see her."

"Colleen's your mom. I want my own mom." She stood and stomped across the room towards me. Her face was red and her hands were balled up in fists. She charged past me and out the front door. Trevor came down the stairs in jeans and a T-shirt. He peered out the doorway Kailyn had left wide open. He smiled and teased, "What did you say this time, Deri?"

"She was searching for your mom's phone number. I told her it wasn't going to be in that phone book. I offered to take her to talk to my mom, and she got mad."

Jim walked up behind us, wiping his hands on a dishtowel.

"Sorry I made her storm off. I was just trying to help."

"It's not your fault," Jim said. "She's been asking about her mom for a couple weeks now."

"Don't cave." Trevor glared at his dad, then bent over to put on his boots.

Jim frowned the same way Trevor did when he was worried. "A girl needs a mom to talk to sometimes."

"Yeah, she needs a mom, not Lorraine. Don't call her."

Jim sighed, then looked at me. "You look pretty, Deri. Are you going on a date or something?"

I glanced at Trevor to see how he reacted. His expression didn't give me any indication as to how he felt about the use of the word "date". It seemed more like he was waiting to see how I was going to react to the use of the word date. "Uh. Trevor and I were going to Vancouver for dinner and to see a play. But an emergency came up with one of my friends, so I had to cancel."

Jim smiled and his left eyebrow jumped up. "Oh, that's too bad. Maybe some other time." He grinned at Trevor before he stepped forward to lean his head out the doorway. "Kailyn! Dinner's ready." He turned, and his eyes darted back and forth between Trevor and me in an amused way. "Do you kids want some dinner?"

"Thanks for the offer, but I'm on my way to Sophie's."

Trevor moved to let Kailyn come back inside, then he stepped out onto the porch. "Save me some. I'm just going to drive Deri to Squamish."

Because I could imagine what Jim was thinking, I avoided eye contact with him and followed Trevor.

"Have fun," Jim said under his breath before the door closed behind us. Trevor was already at the 4Runner, holding the front door open for me.

"Thanks." I hopped in. He walked around the back of the truck and then slid into the driver's seat. "Sorry I upset your sister."

"It's not your fault."

"Maybe you should let her call your mom."

"No." He turned out onto the highway and headed north.

"Why?"

"I said no."

"It's been a long time. Maybe Lorraine has changed."

He shook his head and focused on the road. "I'm not letting her anywhere near Kailyn."

"She's her mom. Don't you think Kailyn should have a say in it?"

"No," he grumbled.

"Why?"

"Because I said so."

He was infuriating when he acted like his dad. So rigid, and kind of bossy. "Who made it your job to make decisions for Kailyn?"

"Lorraine did. When she left." He reached forward to turn up the radio. Another one of the annoying habits he picked up from his dad—avoid talking about anything that's even remotely emotional.

"Just because you're mad at your mom doesn't mean Kailyn shouldn't get to have a relationship with her," I shouted over the volume of the music.

"Drop it, Deri." His jaw muscles tensed and his hands clenched the steering wheel.

The conversation wasn't going to go anywhere. Not wanting to piss him off more, I didn't say anything for the rest of the ride. When he pulled up in front of Sophie's house, he sat back and turned his head to look at me. Then he did something his dad would have never done. "Sorry. I know you were just trying to help, but you don't know everything about my mom. Just trust me on this one."

Relieved to leave each other on good terms, I said. "Okay. I'm sorry too." I pulled the handle and pushed the door open. I fixated on the pavement below me and worked up the courage to say the next part. "I'm also really sorry about ruining our date. Maybe we can try it again sometime." I hopped out and closed the door before he would have a chance to respond and correct me on the fact that it wasn't officially a date.

I ran up to Sophie's door and knocked. She answered, wearing an extra-large, baggy T-shirt like a dress. Her hair was tied in a messy bun, and her eyes were swollen and red. She lunged forward and hugged me. "I'm sorry I was such a bitch. I was upset and angry about my parents and took it out on you."

"I'm sorry I lied to you. It won't ever happen again."

79

"I wasn't really mad at you. My dad lied to my mom about where he'd been. That's why they've been fighting. It was easier to blame you. I'm so sorry. I can't live without you." She released me from the hug and looked at how I was dressed. "Did you have plans?"

"Trevor and I were supposed to go to Vancouver for dinner and a play."

"Shut. Up. Trevor as in Trevor Maverty Trevor?"

I turned and waved at him. He flashed the headlights, then backed out of the driveway.

"Damn, Deri. If I knew you scored a date with the God of the mountain men, I wouldn't have asked you to come here."

"It probably wasn't really a date. I'm glad you called." I wrapped my arm across her shoulder and clung to her as we stepped into the house. "Let's get this girls' night started."

CHAPTER TWELVE

Sophie was a wreck for a couple of weeks after her parents announced they were officially separating. She and I spent a lot of time together, talking. Avoiding her own house, she came down to Britannia on the days Doug was busy and hung out with me while I worked at the front desk. I also did her homework for a while because she couldn't concentrate, and she didn't care if she failed. The insurance company hadn't completed the review of our claim, but the renos had to be finished regardless of who paid for it, so the contractors were still on site every day. I avoided discussing anything to do with the Inn with my granddad. Unfortunately, I could tell by the phone messages from the bank and real-estate agent that the sale was obviously in the works. My homelessness appeared to be imminent.

Trevor didn't ask me out again. Obviously, he hadn't intended it to be a date. Or, he was hurt by the fact that I chose to support Sophie instead of going out with him. But probably not. He would have told me to go to her if I had asked his opinion. Loyalty was a big deal to him. Helping people was an even bigger deal. He would have definitely been disappointed in me if I chose a play over a friend in need. I knew I made the right choice, but I still felt horrible about the golden opportunity I had to give up.

Steve asked me out a lot. We went for coffee a couple times a week. He drove me home so I wouldn't have to take the bus. He also asked me to do other things like dinner, a movie, and snow-shoeing, but I turned him down for everything except coffee. I wasn't sure if I wasn't into more than a friendship with him because I wasn't ready, or if it was because I clung to the ridiculous hope that another chance with Trevor might come up.

In November, the student council organized a collection for the local food bank. We held it on a Saturday. Steve couldn't make it because he was visiting the hospital in the morning and had plans to play hockey with friends in the afternoon. I took Kailyn with me to help. Her job was to tell the volunteers which area they were assigned to. My job was to sort the food items the public dropped off. The second volunteer to show up was Mason and, to my horror, I became tongue-tied in his presence. He was dressed more casually than he ever did for school, in beat-up jeans and an Abercrombie zip-up sweatshirt. Kailyn grinned at him for a second, then remembered her job. "Who are you?"

"Mason Cartwright."

Oh, God. Even his voice was dreamy. Kailyn scanned the list with her finger until she found his name. "You're supposed to load the truck. Go there." She pointed to the back doors of the gym, where a truck was backed in with a ramp set up.

"Thanks." He glanced over at me. My mouth widened in a strange motion that I could only pray resembled something close to a polite smile and not the grimace of someone suffering the discomfort of gas.

"You're cuter than Austin Sullivan," Kailyn said matter-of-factly.

He ran his finger over his eyebrow in an embarrassed way and quietly said, "Um, thanks. Too bad I don't sing as well as he does."

Kailyn agreed and chattered with him about music and some movie Austin starred in. Apparently, I was the only person on the planet who hadn't heard of the guy. Kailyn had always been a good judge of character. If she didn't like someone, she didn't speak at all. The fact that Mason had her engaged and laughing was both impressive and interesting. Attractive, willing to spend his Saturday volunteering, polite and seemingly friendly—I debated what his flaws might be. Nobody was perfect, but none of his imperfections were immediately obvious.

They ended their conversation and I watched him walk to the back of the gym. He took off his sweatshirt and hung it on the back of a chair. His shoulders were not as broad as Trevor's, but he was fit in a slim way. Watching him lift flats of cans into the truck became an instant spectator sport for every other girl, and one or two boys. It was probably only the handsome, mysterious, new kid cliché that had everyone hooked, but I had to admit he intrigued me.

"Do you want to marry him?" Kailyn asked me.

"Who?"

"Mason Cartwright."

I chuckled that she noticed me gawking like a groupie. "No. He's cute, but I'd rather marry Austin Sullivan."

"Trevor looks like Austin. You can just marry Trevor instead."

Yeah. I would have been happy with another invite to wing night at Rusty's with the Search and Rescue guys. Marriage wasn't even on the radar. "Who do you want to marry?"

"Evan."

"Is he a singer or a movie star?"

"Gah! Derian. You're so silly. He's my friend. He works at the library and goes to the centre with me."

"Oh. I didn't know you had a boyfriend." Apparently she was correct when she assessed I wouldn't be of much use to her.

She doodled a Hello Kitty in the margin of the job assignment list. "He's not my boyfriend. He's just a boy who's a friend."

"Does Trevor know you have a boy who's a friend?"

"Yes. He made Evan go out for lunch with us. He asked him lots of questions and embarrassed me. I got mad at him after."

"He was just trying to make sure Evan is a nice guy."

She added the bow and whiskers to her drawing. "I can tell if someone is nice all by myself."

"I know." I took a donation and sorted it as Kailyn directed two more volunteers. "Trevor does the same thing to me, if it makes you feel any better," I added after it quieted down again. "He makes sure the boys I date are nice too."

"Trevor should date you."

I nodded but didn't say anything. As I went back to sorting, I couldn't help but wonder if he had ever mentioned the idea of us dating in front of her. I was tempted to ask her, but the answer was obvious. If he wanted to date we would be dating.

It was late in the afternoon before it quieted down enough for me to talk to Kailyn again. I sat down and said, "You know, my mom kind of left me too. I know how you're feeling. Sometimes I want to talk about girl things, and she's not here, so I have to talk to my friends. You and I are friends. I would be happy to listen whenever you want to talk about things, like boys or whatever."

"Does your mom hug you?"

"When I see her she does."

"Then, you don't know how it feels."

Struck by how sad she sounded, I wasn't sure what to say.

Randomly she asked, "Where are you going to live when the Inn gets torn down to make a new hotel?"

"What? Where did you hear that?"

"From the man in the suit who has meetings with your grandpa."

That blow hit me in the gut. I stared at her for a while, then said, "I don't know." It made me angry to know it was happening whether I liked it or not and whether my dad would have liked it or not. It seemed like such a waste to do all the renos only to tear it down. I turned around and threw soup cans one at a time into a tote. I fired each shot with progressive aggression. After a dozen, I was chucking them like a baseball pitcher, and the tote rebounded loudly against the gym wall with each impact. The tins got dented, but I didn't care.

"Um, Deri," a female voice said behind me. I turned, realizing how unstable I must have looked. It was a classmate named Jane. She stared at me to gauge my volatility, then said, "We're shutting down the donations for the day. Mr. Orton wants everyone to shift over to load the trucks."

"Okay thanks." I placed the tin gently down on the table to appear at least partly normal.

Kailyn and I carried the last tub over to the parking lot exit, where the other trucks were parked. Mason happened to be standing in the doorway but stepped aside to let us pass. There was something intense about the way he looked at me. Not creepy. Not flirty either. Just penetrating. Based on the size of his fan club at school, it must have been how he looked at all females. Not that I kept tabs on him, exactly. God, he smelled good.

"Hey, Deri," Trevor said, startling me.

I blinked and tried to zone back into reality. "Oh. Hi. Is it five o'clock already?"

"Yeah." He shoved my shoulder playfully. "You look wiped. Are you guys ready to go home?"

"Not quite yet. Sorry. There was a better response from the community than we anticipated."

"What can I do to help?"

"The last truck still needs to be loaded. If you don't mind."

He nodded and walked over to help Mason and two other guys. About half an hour later, they shook hands and Trevor made his way back over to where Kailyn and I were taking down the tables. "The new kid seems like your type," he said to me. "Does Steve have a little competition on his hands?"

Mason was everybody's type, but that was irrelevant. "Steve and I are just friends. We go out for coffee to talk about his sister—that's it." I picked up my bag and coat, and we all walked out the side door of the school gym.

"So, you like the new kid?"

"What?"

He laughed. "Evan, Steve, and now Mason Cartwright. I'm going to know everything about every guy in town if you two keep this pace up."

I angled my eyebrows and glared at him, not because he was doing background checks again, but because he didn't want to be on the list of potential suitors. "It's rude to interrogate someone you don't even know about their personal life, don't you think?"

Unaffected by my visual daggers, he squeezed his arm around his sister as we crossed the parking lot towards the 4Runner. "Don't worry. We were only making small talk. He had no idea he was being screened."

"Even if Mason were a candidate, which he's not, I'd prefer if you stopped interfering in my life," I snapped. Apparently I was wiped, and grumpy about the Inn being sold, and irked by the undeniable proof that I had been delusional when I read too much into Trevor's dinner and play offer.

"Yeah!" Kailyn said defiantly. "You're not the boss of us."

His expression turned serious. "I know I'm not the boss of you, but if anything happened to either of you, I wouldn't be able to live with myself." He opened the passenger doors for us. We both stood staring at him.

He looked really hurt. I felt bad that I took my bad mood out on him, so before I climbed into the back seat, I said, "Sorry. I know you do it because you care. Thank you."

Kailyn wrapped her arms around his waist and said, "I'm sorry too. You're the best brother in the whole wide world."

He kissed the top of her head, then helped her climb in and put her seatbelt on. As he was doing that, a vision flicked through my mind.

A row of headlights shone on ice. Then it was pitch black and freezing cold. I was in the water and couldn't breathe. I swam up and hit ice from beneath. My hands ran along the smooth surface, searching for an opening. I couldn't find it.

My vision ended and I gasped for air as if I had actually been drowning.

Trevor stood by the open passenger door and studied my expression. "What did you see?"

I shook my head, about to deny seeing anything, but it seemed so vivid. So real. "Someone fell through the ice."

He closed Kailyn's door and walked around the front of the truck to get in the driver's side. "Could you tell where?"

I closed my eyes to concentrate. "I don't know, but it seemed familiar. Around here somewhere. I can't even guess when."

Trevor turned on the engine and pulled out of the parking lot. I had read the intuition book he gave me. Twice. At the end of every chapter, the practice exercises were designed to fine-tune natural intuition. The goal was to observe whatever popped up without analyzing or attempting to attach meaning to it. Just observe. Don't force anything. Unfortunately, I hadn't had any strong intuitions since Giselle's accident, so I hadn't tested it yet. The fact that the visions were only coming before a serious event worried me. I missed the old days when I was only predicting pop quizzes and telephone rings before they happened. I exhaled and tried to relax my mind to see more details like a face or a vehicle or a place. I saw a hockey game.

"Oh my God!" I gasped.

"What?" Trevor glanced over his shoulder at me.

"Steve and his friends are playing hockey on Skawnee Lake. What if it was one of them?"

"It's on the way home. We can go by there and check it out if you want."

"Okay. Hurry."

CHAPTER THIRTEEN

It took fifteen minutes to get to the turnoff that accessed the rocky logging road to Skawnee Lake. About ten cars were lined up on the shore. The headlights lit a makeshift hockey rink. We pulled up at the end of the row and parked. Everyone was safe and sound. The guys looked like they were having fun.

Trevor turned off the engine but left the headlights on. "What else did you see?"

"The headlights and someone trapped under the ice." I sat forward, anxious because it did all feel familiar.

"The ice is thick enough for playing hockey. Maybe it happens some other time in the future."

"Yeah. Sorry." Partly relieved that nobody was in danger and partly disappointed that the vagueness of my intuition had let me down again, I rested my chin on Kailyn's seat back. "I've been doing the exercises in the book you gave me. Apparently, it isn't helping my accuracy that much."

He smiled as if he was proud of me for at least trying.

"I'm cold," Kailyn complained.

Trevor turned on the engine and cranked the heat for her. Each of the guys left the ice and threw their hockey gear into their trucks. A couple of vehicles backed out and disappeared down the logging road, so Trevor shifted the 4Runner into reverse to leave. A Jeep spun its tires. Then the driver four-wheeled over the rocks of the lake shore. Two other trucks followed, and the three of them spun around doing doughnuts on the ice.

"Idiots. The ice isn't thick enough for that," Trevor said and leapt out of the truck.

"No, no, no," I repeated. Panic surged as I realized one of them was about to live through what I'd seen.

The driver of the Jeep gunned it and drove out towards the middle of the lake. He obviously pulled the hand brake to spin the Jeep in three-sixties. Guys from the shore yelled at him to stop screwing around, but he either couldn't hear them or didn't care.

Trevor stood in front of the 4Runner and watched the three trucks race around on the lake. My eyes were locked on Trevor when a horrendous cracking echoed through the valley. It was literally thunderous as it bounced off the surrounding mountains. The Jeep dropped and disappeared into the lake. The two other trucks gunned it back towards shore.

Trevor ran and opened the back of the 4Runner. I got out of the truck as he grabbed some ropes and put on a life vest. "Call 911 and tell them a vehicle is submerged in the lake with a person trapped inside."

I tried not to sound hysterical as I followed his instructions and told the 911 operator what was happening. She had to tell me to calm down three times. My voice kept getting high-pitched and super-speeded up as I watched Trevor. He walked out onto the ice, then slid along his stomach as he got close to the gaping black hole.

Fortunately, Kailyn was engrossed in one of her magazines, unaware of what was going on. I took deep breaths to try to calm down, for Kailyn's sake, but it wasn't working. I rushed over to where all the other guys stood on the shore. "How many people were in the Jeep?" I asked Steve.

"Derian? What are you doing here?"

"I'll explain later. How many people were in the Jeep?"

"Just Luke."

I relayed the information to the operator, then ran back to Trevor's truck to get a blanket. The rope Trevor had set up stretched between the bumper of his truck and his waist. It pulled tight as he leaned forward and thrust his arm into the water repeatedly. It was taking too long—he couldn't find him.

I ran, gave my phone to Steve, and told him to talk to the 911 operator. The intuition book mentioned that physical touch on a significant object could sometimes aid with the clarity of a vision. Eager to help, I stepped tentatively onto the ice, pressed my hands flat against the cold surface and closed my eyes. In the vision, the hole in the ice was to Luke's left. "Reach your right hand out," I yelled as Trevor dipped his lower body into the water.

Trevor glanced up at me, and with the same trusting expression he had when I showed up on a sunny day in my snowsuit, he leaned sideways to his right. He moved in a jerky way and finally, with one arm, he yanked a body halfway out of the water. Trevor grabbed his belt and heaved him again, flinging him farther onto the ice along his stomach.

Trevor pulled himself out of the water by inching his hands along the rope. Then he edged on his stomach across the slick surface and pulled Luke by the collar of his jacket away from the hole. Luke looked as if he wasn't moving on his own. Trevor had to keep dragging him as they made their way across the ice a few feet at a time. When they got close to shore, a couple of other guys ventured out onto the ice and carried Luke the rest of the way.

Trevor stood and scrambled up onto the rocks. I wrapped the blanket around Luke and watched as Trevor rolled up his ropes and headed back to the truck. He took off his wet clothes and got another blanket for himself. As the ambulance and Fire Rescue truck arrived, Trevor hopped into the 4Runner. Two of the firefighters were friends of Trevor's dad, so I wandered over and told them what I witnessed as the paramedics attended to Luke. A police officer arrived and also interviewed me before I walked over to Trevor's window to check on him. He rolled it down. His lips were blue and he was shivering. Kailyn was asleep in the passenger seat.

"Fire Rescue wants to talk to you."

"Who is it?"

"Pete and Frank. Are you okay?"

"No. I feel like punching Luke in the face for being such a jackass. I can't go near him."

"Stay warm. I'll tell Pete to come over here."

I sent Pete to talk to Trevor and watched as the ambulance took Luke away. Steve stood next to me and wrapped his arm across my shoulders. "Here's your phone."

"Thanks."

"That rescue was really impressive. It was lucky Trevor was here. Why were you here?"

"Um." I searched for an answer that sounded plausible, since *I saw it happen before it happened* was not something I wanted to advertise—not that he'd believe the truth anyway. "Trevor had to get something from one of the guys. I don't know. I didn't ask."

He frowned because I was a bad liar. Fortunately, he didn't call me on it. "How did the food drive go?"

"Great. We filled all the trucks."

He stared at me as if he still thought it was curious that Trevor and I randomly showed up at precisely the right time.

To avoid having to answer more questions about our unbelievable timing, I said, "Trevor must be cold. I should probably get going. I'll see you at school on Monday. We can go for coffee if you want."

"Okay. See ya." He hugged me, then got into his truck and backed out.

Pete was still talking to Trevor, so I walked over and stood next to him. "You better get home and warm up," he said to Trevor. "Bye Derian. Take care of him."

"Sure."

Pete walked away. Trevor pulled the blanket tighter around his shoulders. His teeth chattered and his body convulsed with each shiver.

"Do you want me to drive?"

He laughed. "No. You only have your learner's permit. I want to make it home alive."

"Ha ha. I'm not that bad of a driver."

"I just need to warm up some more. Get in quick and close the door." He rolled up the window.

I opened the back door but didn't get in. I took my coat off and threw it into the backseat. Then I stripped off my sweater, my T-shirt, and then my thermal underwear top. Kicking my boots off one foot at a time, I shimmied out of my jeans and threw all the layers into the back before closing the door. I stood outside his door in only my underwear and boots. My turquoise push-up bra actually matched the turquoise-and-white-striped boy shorts I was wearing. It wasn't a super sexy look, but it wasn't shabby either, which was good enough since the point of the strip down was to prevent hypothermia, not seduce him. He stared at me through the window. His expression was indecipherable, as if he wasn't sure what to think. I reached my arm forward and pulled the handle.

"What are you doing?" he asked as the door swung open.

"Saving your life." I moved his arms to open the blanket and climbed into the truck to sit sideways on his lap. I crammed my legs in tightly until I could shut the door. He wrapped the blanket around my body to cover us both. Although I hadn't meant for it to be, it was the most suggestive thing I had ever done. He didn't seem to mind, so I worked up enough courage to run my hands across his chest and down his abs. "You feel like ice."

92

"Mmm." He blinked slowly. "Who taught you to strip down to save someone from freezing to death?"

"You did."

He bit his lip as if he wanted to prevent himself from speaking. After a very sexy pause, he smiled and ran his hand over the curve of my waist. "Well, we wouldn't want me to die, would we?"

"No, we wouldn't want that." I kept moving my hands over his skin, which made it warmer inside our blanket tent. I moved to rest my cheek against his and let my lips linger close to his neck so he would feel the warmth of my breath. I arched my back a little to press my chest snug against his. He tensed his arms and pulled me even tighter. It made my heart alternate between racing and missing beats, as if it were malfunctioning.

When I slipped the fingers of my right hand through his wet hair, he closed his eyes. His shivers disappeared as I ran my other hand up his arm, over his muscular bicep, and back across his chest. He opened his eyes and stared at me. His lips parted slightly.

Kailyn woke up and pointed at us accusingly with a big grin on her face. "Hey. Are you guys going to kiss?"

I smiled and waited. Our faces were literally centimetres apart.

He leaned his forehead against mine and inhaled slowly. "No, Kiki, we're not going to kiss," he finally said. "She's just keeping me warm."

I didn't mind too much that he said no, because it seemed by the way he said it, that maybe no wasn't what he wanted to say. I ran my hands down his arms and curled my body to rest my cheek on his shoulder.

"You did it," he whispered and his breath tickled my neck.

"Did what?"

"Your vision saved him. He would have probably died if we weren't here."

I shook my head to disagree. "You saved him. I just stood around and watched you being amazingly brave."

93

"I wouldn't have been here if it weren't for you."

"That actually makes me feel worse. It means I could have prevented my dad's death if I had known to stop him from driving that day."

He exhaled heavily before he spoke again. "Maybe there are some things in life that are meant to be changed and some things that aren't. Everything happens for a reason, Deri."

Tears built up along my eyelids. "I wish it didn't happen."

"I know." He kissed the top of my head, which felt so comforting. "We make a good team." His hand slid slowly over my hip and down the outside of my thigh.

"I'm hungry. Let's go," Kailyn said impatiently.

I lifted my head to look at Trevor, wondering if being a good team could have multiple meanings. His cheeks were rosy from the heat that radiated off his body.

He smiled. "Thanks. I think I'm warm enough to drive home now." He moved his arms and opened the blanket to let me out of our little cocoon. After a reluctant pause, I twisted and crawled over the console into the back of the truck. I put my jeans back on, and when I looked up he was watching me in the rearview mirror. I didn't know what any of it meant, but it was the best feeling in the world.

CHAPTER FOURTEEN

Trevor never mentioned anything about the hypothermia incident after it happened. I hoped it had maybe propelled our relationship to the next level—obviously it hadn't. He seemed to only think of it as a lifesaving technique with benefits. To me, it was more than that, and I couldn't stop thinking about how it felt to touch his bare skin. I was pretty much obsessed. I asked Sophie for advice on how to handle it in case I got another opportunity. She said if sitting on his lap in my underwear didn't do the trick, I was a lost cause. She did, however, suggest I might have been more successful if I had attempted it without his sister sleeping right beside us.

In early December, a guy wearing a suit walked into the Inn. I was stationed at the front desk, reading. "May I help you?"

One side of his mouth lifted, but not exactly like a smile. "You must be Derian."

I figured he was one of the developers, so I acted cold. "How may I help you?"

He reached his arm out to shake my hand. I just stared at him, leaving him hanging. He eventually withdrew the handshake offer and said, "My name's Bill Waddell. I've been working with your grandpa on a deal for the Inn."

I studied his eyes and tried to place him. I'd heard that name before, but his face wasn't familiar at all. "Waddell?"

"That's right." He opened the end of an architect tube and pulled out a roll of papers. "Would you like to take a look at the preliminary designs we're proposing for the development?"

"No thanks, Mr. Waddell. I wouldn't want to waste your time."

He chuckled in a way that made it clear he found me more than a nuisance. "Listen, kid. You can pout and stomp your feet all you want, but the facts are that your grandpa has debts he can't pay off unless he sells the place, and the only reason anyone would buy an old building like this is to redevelop the land. Grow up."

Waddell. I remembered where I'd heard the name before. It was the name on the insurance document. The guy who had sent the rejection letter—Len or Ken or something. "Do you have any brothers, Mr. Waddell?"

He shook his head in a confused and impatient way. "I have two brothers. Why?"

I frowned as the pieces clicked together. "Just wondering." I went back to reading my book, hoping he would leave. If he and his brother were working together on a scam, it would explain why the insurance investigation was taking unreasonably long.

"Is your grandpa here?"

"Nope." I stood, prepared to walk away to end the interaction.

"When do you expect him back?"

"Hard to say."

"Could you call him, please?"

"The reception in the mountain is sketchy. I'll give him the message that you dropped by." I smiled at him in an artificially sweet way.

He lifted his eyebrow, not impressed with my attitude, and placed the architect tube on the desk. "Take a look at the drawings. This place costs a fortune to run, and the renovations add up to more than your grandpa will ever be able to earn back unless he sells. You don't seem like the kind of girl who would want an old man to die exhausted and penniless. You might as well get on board."

"Goodbye, Mr. Waddell." I pretended to read, but I was so angry. Okay, yeah, it was completely selfish to expect my granddad to work himself into bankruptcy just so I wouldn't have to let go of my childhood memories, but if the Inn needed to be sold, I didn't want it to be to a slime ball who was potentially trying to take advantage of my granddad. The bells on the door jingled as he left.

Once his car pulled out onto the highway, I Googled his name and found everything I could about the development company. Then I called Doug, "Hey, I emailed you some information about the developer who wants to tear down the Inn and build a resort. Can you find out if he's related to the Waddell at the insurance agency who denied our claim? I'm worried they might be working together to force Granddad to sell."

"Sure. I'll take a look and get back to you."

"Thanks." My granddad's car drove by the window, so I rushed out to the parking lot and helped him carry the grocery bags in. "Mr. Waddell came by while you were out and dropped off the architect's drawings," I said as we entered through the side door to the kitchen.

Granddad placed the canvas bags on the counter and turned to face me. "Are you ready to talk about the sale now?"

I had no choice. "Did you know that the guy from the insurance company who rejected our claim for the flood is also a Waddell?"

His white caterpillar eyebrows angled together. "I'm sure it's just a coincidence."

"What if it's not? What if they're working together to force you to sell?"

He shook his head and loaded groceries into the fridge. "We need to sell eventually, Derian." He turned to face me, and he looked so tired. "I can't keep doing this forever."

I glanced around the kitchen, remembering my dad making pancakes, my grandma rolling out the dough for cinnamon buns, and Trevor and me playing hide-and-seek. Holding onto the Inn wasn't going to bring any of those things back from the past. I knew that, but it was hard to accept it. I crossed the kitchen and hugged him. "Okay."

CHAPTER FIFTEEN

Doug got back to me after doing some digging around. The Waddells were brothers, and several of their businesses had gone bankrupt in the past. They'd also been sued twelve times for not paying creditors. Although I had decided to accept the sale of the Inn because it was what was best for my granddad, I convinced him to do some more investigation before committing to a business deal with the Waddells.

Two weeks later, Granddad was seated by the fireplace in the library, the blueprints spread out on the table, where I had always played board games with my dad. "Hi, sweetheart. Do you want to take a look at these?"

I leaned over his shoulder and peeked. It was a gorgeous resort. But nothing could adequately replace the Inn, as far as I was concerned.

He reached up to his shoulder and patted my hand. "The insurance company has handed the investigation over to the police fraud department. They are going to reimburse us for everything."

"Really? That's great." I kissed his cheek and then sat down in my dad's leather chair.

Granddad smiled, and for the first time since the flood happened, he relaxed. "Don't get too excited, though. The Inn is still on the market. If the right developer or buyer comes along, I'm going to consider it."

"I know." I leaned back and crossed my feet on the ottoman. I ran my hand over the worn leather of the armrest. My dad sat in the chair to read every night after dinner. The roughness was a physical reminder that he had once existed. It always comforted me. "Sorry I was being difficult. I know you can't run the business forever. I'm just having a hard time letting go of my dad."

Granddad nodded and reached over to pat my hand again.

Just before Christmas, Steve dropped me off at the Inn after one of our coffee talks. He turned the engine off, then looked at me as if he wanted to say something. He exhaled heavily to prepare. "I want you to know how much I appreciate you being here for me."

"Any time," I said.

Without a hesitation he blurted out, "Do you want to go on a real date?"

"Uh." I shifted in the seat and sat up straighter. The sparks with Trevor, although they had all fizzled out, were more exciting to me than the feelings I had for Steve. As much of a long shot as it was for something to maybe happen with Trevor, I did still hope for it. And I wanted to be available in case the opportunity came up. "I'm not sure about dating. I don't want to do anything that would jeopardize our friendship."

"I really like you, and I hope we can be more than friends."

I stared out the side window in the direction of Trevor's house, wondering how I would feel if nothing encouraging had ever happened between us. It was snowing and the flakes melted when they hit the glass. I traced my finger along the trail it left when the droplets slid down, not sure how to respond.

"I know you like Trevor, but—"

"What?" I gawked at him, mouth open.

He fidgeted with his keys. "It's pretty obvious you like Trevor, but it seems like something would have already happened between you two if he wanted it to."

I was so angry. Not because I thought it was mean for Steve to say that, but because he was right. He winced as if he regretted bringing it up, but I didn't blame him. At least he had the guts to put it out there and tell me how he felt. With impeccable timing, the 4Runner pulled off the highway and parked. Trevor climbed out and looked at Steve's Explorer. I needed to get some guts. I also needed time to figure everything out before I could give Steve an answer. I focused my attention back on him and said, "I'm leaving tomorrow to stay with my mom. I'll call you when I get back. We can talk about it then, if that's okay."

"Sure." He looked disappointed, which I wasn't sure how to respond to. Before I turned to get out of the truck, he pulled my elbow towards him. "One more thing before you go." With one finger he tilted my chin up, stared into my eyes briefly, and then pressed his lips against mine. I felt something a little surprising rush through me. Since it was my first proper kiss, I kissed him back as he moved his hand to cradle my neck. It felt good, but I wasn't sure if I wanted it to, so I pulled away. "Sorry," he said.

"It's fine. I have to go." I jumped out of his truck and ran through the snow to the front door.

The next morning, I was packing and getting ready to take the bus to Vancouver when my phone buzzed with a text. It was from Trevor: *Can we talk before you leave?*

Excited and nervous at the same time, I wrote back: *Sure. Come over.* There was a knock at my bedroom door as soon as the message sent. I knew it was him because he used to always text me while he was already standing in the hall. "What took you so long," I joked, and let him in.

He shrugged and smiled. His gaze moved around the room. It received a minor makeover along with the rest of the rooms on the first floor, so I decided to redecorate. It was the first time

Trevor had been in it since I moved back in after they finished the renovations. "I like what you've done with the place. It looks more grown up." He stood in front of my dresser and slid the picture of us at his graduation out of the mirror frame. He studied it for a second, then tucked it back in.

I watched as he crossed the room, flopped down on my bed, and hugged my favourite doll from when I was little. He crossed his feet at his ankles, bent one arm behind his head, and stared at me in a weird way.

"What?" I asked.

"I've missed you."

My heart did something unnatural, even though I refused to let myself believe he meant he missed me in a romantic way. I glanced at him and took a mental picture of him lying on my bed. I needed a bigger bed. He pretty much took up all the space. There wouldn't be much room for me to join him if he ever asked.

"So, you and Rawlings are getting hot and heavy, eh?"

"No."

"It looked like it was pretty steamy in his truck yesterday."

Oh God. I didn't even want to imagine what he thought was going on. "You shouldn't be spying."

"I wasn't spying. You were going at it in a parking lot. Everyone could see."

"We weren't going at it. There was nothing to see."

He reached into his jacket pocket and pulled out a flat wrapped gift with a bow on it. "Merry Christmas."

Confused that he was giving it to me early, I didn't reach to take it from him. "Why don't you just bring it to my mom's place on Christmas?"

"I can't come this year."

"What?" I didn't mean to sound as desperately devastated as I was. "But our families always have Christmas together. It's tradition."

"I have to work until eight. If your mom came up to Britannia it would work, but since everyone is going down to Vancouver, it'll be too late by the time I get there."

"But it's Christmas. Can't you change your shift?"

"I'm the low guy on the totem pole. I don't have a choice."

Bummed, I sat down on the edge of my mattress beside his hip. I had to take really deep breaths to hold the tears back. He reached his arm around in front of me and placed the gift on my lap.

"What is it?" I asked, trying to hide my disappointment.

"A surprise. You have to wait until Christmas to open it."

His gift was in my desk, so I stood and walked over to open the drawer. I wrapped it nicely because it wasn't a very fancy gift. "Please remember when you open this that I don't have an income, and I spent the hundred dollars that Murphy gave me to get their house cleaned. It's the thought that counts."

"Getting their house cleaned was a gift for me too since I hang out there." He reached over to take the present from me.

I sat on the floor and rested my back against my bed so he wouldn't see my expression.

He swept his finger to tuck my hair behind my ear and away from my face "I'm sorry I can't make it this year."

"Me too." I exhaled to steady my voice. "Will your dad and Kailyn still come?"

"For sure."

I turned to face him. "But then you'll be here all alone."

"It's just for dinner. I'll be at work anyway. It's no big deal."

"Yeah, no big deal." I looked away again and pulled my knees into my chest.

The mattress shifted as he sat up and swung his legs over the edge beside me. "I've got to go to work." He leaned and kissed the top of my head. "Did you notice what I did with the tiles under your sink?"

I shook my head, too sad to care about stupid tiles.

"Have a good time at your mom's. I'll see you when you get back."

"Bye," I mumbled.

He left, and the cry I'd been holding in flooded out. They weren't just tears about Trevor not coming for Christmas. They were also angry tears that the reason he couldn't come was because my mom was breaking the tradition and forcing us all to go to Vancouver instead of her coming up to Britannia. Neither she nor I felt like celebrating the first Christmas after my dad had died, but at least she came up on the train and we all spent time together remembering him. Celebrating at the apartment without my dad or Trevor felt all wrong.

Then, as if she knew I was livid with her, she called. "Hi sweetheart. Are you on the way out? You don't want to miss the bus. It's the only one coming down today. Everything is ready for you. I'm so excited. You don't need to bring any toiletries. I stocked your bathroom with all your favourite products. It's going to be so much fun. Wear your boots and a scarf. And gloves. It's cold."

It took all my effort to sound cordial, but I knew I had to since starting off the next two weeks with her on the wrong foot would only make me more miserable. "Okay, Mom. I'll see you soon. I should go. I don't want to miss the bus."

After saying goodbye, I dragged my butt off the floor. Although I was dreading the visit, I couldn't leave my mom all alone on Christmas. Splashing cold water on my face stopped the tears but not the horrible beat-up feeling in my chest. The towel slid off the rack and puddled on the floor. When I crouched to pick it up, I noticed the tiles under the sink. Trevor had replaced some of the white mosaic tiles with cream-coloured ones and it spelled out LAFLEUR. It was so beautiful.

I texted to thank him, then wandered out to the highway and waited for the bus. It was packed with cheery people, all their bulky winter coats, luggage, and parcels. They were all in a festive and chatty mood, which only irritated me more.

By the time I walked from the Vancouver station to my mom's apartment, I was officially depressed. She did an amazing job decorating the apartment for the holidays, but it didn't look like all my other Christmases growing up. Her colour theme was blue, white, and silver—a sparkling winter wonderland everywhere, including the bathrooms. The tree was made of silver tinsel and covered in baby white lights. Every one of the decorations was encrusted in glitter. She went all out because she felt guilty for not coming up to Britannia to see me. I wasn't convinced the effort made up for everything.

I sat in the living room for two days wrapped in a blanket, staring at the twinkling tree, eating chocolates, and drinking hot apple cider until I nearly made myself sick. Fortunately, she went to work during the day, so I had the place to myself. When she was home, I avoided meaningful conversations and her inadvertent nit-picking by watching movies, taking long baths, or hanging out in my room listening to music.

Trevor was right. There were worse moms in the world than mine but mine was a lawyer and liked to argue her case for everything. It didn't matter if she was wrong, she still argued until you started to believe maybe she was right. Which was a brilliant talent in the court room but annoying as hell if you were her daughter. My dad never minded. He would go at it with her, debating his point for as long as he found it amusing. Then he would say something cleverly charming, they would kiss and then disappear into their bedroom. When she and I disagreed, it always ended with me saying, "Okay, you're right."

When she wasn't arguing, she was worrying. To me, it was ironic that she let me live alone with Granddad in Britannia Beach but got antsy if I went down to the pool in her building by myself. She was also convinced I was going to be lured by a pedophile from the internet but wasn't concerned about all the strangers who stayed at the Inn. And, although she knew I made breakfasts for all the guests, she was convinced I was going to blow up the kitchen in the condo every time I made myself lunch. She was irrational sometimes. Everyone else seemed to accept her quirks and deal with them. They drove me crazy.

"Let's go," she called from the foyer on the morning of the third day. She had taken the day off and held up our ice skates. "You need to get out of the house and get some fresh air."

"I'm not in the mood," I moaned.

"The winter air will put you in the mood. Let's go."

Since being cooped up in the condo with her all day didn't appeal to me, I reluctantly got dressed and followed her to the elevator. We walked to the outdoor ice rink at Robson Square. The streets bustled with holiday shoppers and there was a merry vibe. All the shop windows were decked out, and street vendors sold warm chestnuts and mini-doughnuts on every corner.

"So, what has you so depressed?" Mom asked as we laced up our skates.

"I don't know." I inhaled deeply because I didn't want to talk about it with her. It wasn't like we were close like that.

"Boy trouble?"

I didn't answer. I stood up and walked gingerly towards the rink. I nearly fell when I stepped out onto the ice, but she was able to reach her hand out in time to steady me. We skated side by side, counter-clockwise in a big circle. It felt weird because we so rarely did things together.

"I know having Christmas in the city is an adjustment for you, and I appreciate that you're making an effort."

I nodded at the validation, glad that she at least understood why it sucked.

We skated in silence for a while before I finally said, "So, I wouldn't exactly call it boy trouble, but there is a boy who likes me and wants to date." I glanced sideways to see how she would react to my uncharacteristic disclosure of personal information.

"That's a good thing, isn't it?"

"Not really. I like someone else."

"Oooh, drama." Her eyebrows rose in a suggestive way.

"Uh, no. There is no drama. He's not interested in me in a boyfriend-girlfriend way."

A crease formed along her forehead as she thought seriously about my predicament. After we had skated one full rotation around the rink she asked, "What makes you think he doesn't like you in a girlfriend way?"

"We spend a lot of time together, he's single, and he's had lots of opportunity to ask me out if he wanted to. He sort of asked me out once, but I couldn't make it. He hasn't asked again. It's seems like he would have done it by now if he was going to."

"How long have you known him?"

I couldn't tell her I had known him for eleven years because she'd know it was Trevor, so I said, "Years."

"Maybe he's shy?"

"No. He's confident and popular."

"Does he know for sure you're interested?"

"Um, I don't know. It's not like I've flat out told him." I caught an edge. She had to grab my arm to prevent me from falling.

Once I was stable again, she said, "Maybe you should flat out tell him and see what happens."

I glanced at her again and then stared at the ice in front of me as we continued to skate. I wondered if Trevor knew for sure I liked him. It was possible he didn't since I hadn't even realized it myself at first. It was likely that he did, though, since even Steve had picked up on it. Maybe he was unsure since I hung out with Steve too.

"If you're honest with him, the worst that can happen is he'll say he's not interested, and you'll be right back where you are now. You have nothing to lose," she said encouragingly.

"Except my pride."

"Any boy who doesn't realize how special you are doesn't deserve you."

That wasn't the problem with Trevor. He had always treated me like I was special. There was some other reason why he didn't want to date me. Probably a perfectly valid reason like the fact he was planning to go to university in the fall. Or, the fact he knew neither one of us would likely be living in Britannia Beach for much longer. Or, the fact he didn't feel the same way back. It was probably better for my mental health to go back to having no hope.

My mom ended my defeatist internal monologue when she launched into a lecture about safe sex, the preferred choice of abstinence, and gynecological health. It was absolutely torturous, so I cut the skating short to end the misery.

We went out for lunch at a nice restaurant before doing a little Christmas shopping. She was right about my mood improving by getting out of the house, and since she had stopped with the heart-to-heart attempts, we were actually having a pretty good time. I bought an Austin Sullivan poster for Kailyn and hiking socks for her dad. My mom bought me a long red cashmere sweater to wear at dinner. It was too expensive, but she insisted. I already had my mom's and granddad's gifts wrapped back at the apartment. The only other thing I had to buy was an ornament to hang on the tree in memory of my dad. I purposely picked a sparkly one to match her design theme. It was a three-dimensional snowflake that I imagined had floated down from heaven. I cried as I paid for it. The sales clerk seemed equally concerned and uncomfortable.

"Sorry," I mumbled and walked away to find my mom.

CHAPTER SIXTEEN

I slept in on Christmas morning because we always waited to open our gifts until just before dinner. I called Sophie and Steve to wish them a merry Christmas. Sophie was struggling because it was her first Christmas since her parents had separated. We talked until my mom called me for brunch. After we ate, we watched *National Lampoon's Christmas Vacation* on TV. Then I helped her get everything ready for our big turkey dinner.

I had left the scissors on the island, where I'd been wrapping gifts, so I reached over to grab them. When I handed them to her, she seemed perplexed.

"What?" I asked. "You need the scissors, don't you?"

She nodded but still seemed confused. "Yeah. To cut the packaging on the cheese log, which is still in the fridge. How did you—"

I glanced at the counter, where I had seen the cheese log only a few seconds earlier. It wasn't there. Great. The line between my intuition and reality had blurred. If I couldn't tell the difference between a vision and real life, the descent into insanity would be slick and quick.

Her eyebrows rose. "Oh. Wow. You can still do that? I thought you grew out of your little mind-reading ability."

"I can't read minds. I anticipated that you might need scissors. Anyone with basic situational awareness can do that," I said, trying to downplay it.

She studied my expression, contemplating whether to press the subject or let it drop. She was smart enough to know I had used more than just keen observation skills, but to my relief, she turned and opened the fridge to get the cheese log.

When I was ten years old, she tried to convince my dad to have my brain studied at the university, which I assumed would land me in a psychiatric hospital. Fortunately, my dad didn't think it was a good idea to make a big deal about what he considered to be nothing more than sharp instincts. I purposely hid all my intuitions from my mom after that, including the fact that I had seen my dad's accident before it happened. There was no reason for both of us to be haunted by the exact heart-wrenching details of the last moments of his life. Plus, I already blamed myself enough. I couldn't handle how she would look at me if she knew.

"Cut those in all the same size chunks," she said, referring to the carrots I had started to chop.

Frustrated by everything needing to be precisely her way, I said, "They'll still taste the same no matter what size they are."

"Actually, they cook differently if they aren't uniform. The little ones will get dried and burned."

Irritated that she was right, I shook my head and started cutting them all exactly the same size, like a psycho cutting off someone's fingers.

"So, Grandpa still has the Inn on the market."

Really? Was she trying to provoke me while I had a knife in my hand? I moved to the stove and mashed the yams with unnecessary force before I answered. "Yeah."

"Well, when it sells, you can obviously come live with me and finish school down here."

"Sure," I said, because if I debated with her, it was a conversation that would land me right back in my funk and ruin the progress we had made. "Can we talk about something else, please?"

She sighed at how difficult I was to connect with and sprinkled brown sugar on the pulverized yams. "It's too bad Trevor has to work tonight."

"Yeah." I tried to sound nonchalant, even though her attempt to steer the conversation to safer territory had inadvertently hit another land mine. "He's had Christmas dinner with us for the past eleven years. Maybe we need to have it in Britannia again next year."

"Oh, I don't think where we host it matters. He's getting older. He has his own life. Even if I came up on the train, he probably wouldn't want to have dinner with us anymore. It was bound to happen eventually."

An actual gasp escaped from my throat. I covered it up by pretending to cough. It hadn't occurred to me that we'd had our last Christmas with Trevor ever. I had to flatten my palms on the granite countertops to brace myself. It felt like my mom had literally jammed her carving knife into my back. "Excuse me," I sputtered and ducked out to hide in my bedroom.

I sat in the dark on the edge of my bed for a long time, trying to catch my breath. She was right. Especially if Trevor got a serious girlfriend, who wasn't me. We were bound to drift apart for family holidays. Accepting that probably wouldn't have been hard if I hadn't stupidly gone and developed real feelings for him. But I had, and I didn't know how to turn them off.

Eventually, I mustered enough energy to change into black leggings and my new cashmere sweater. I strung my dad's wedding ring from my necklace and clasped it around my neck. After I brushed my hair and applied some make-up, I stood by my window and stared at the snow falling heavily—too heavily. I rushed back into the kitchen.

"Mom, did you see how hard it's snowing? They're not going to be able to drive back up to Britannia if the highway gets closed.

She put down the tray of dinner buns she had just removed

from the oven and walked over to the floor-to-ceiling windows in the living room. The city streets were already coated with thick snow. Big, fluffy flakes still rapidly fell. If it kept snowing that hard through dinner, they would have to stay overnight.

"Well, it makes for a nice cozy Christmas. Kailyn can stay with you, Dad can stay in the guest room, and Jim can stay on the pull-out couch in the den. Do you mind getting the bed linens and towels ready for everyone while I finish with dinner?"

"Sure."

I made up the guest bed and pull-out couch, then stripped the sheets off my bed and put fresh ones on. The doorbell rang as I was getting an extra pillow for Kailyn out of the closet. My mom sang, "Merry Christmas", and familiar voices filled the apartment. I held my breath, closed my eyes, and strained to hear Trevor's voice. I hoped that by some miracle he had gotten off work early and come down with them. I didn't hear him.

My granddad's giggly laugh and Kailyn's singing of *Frosty the Snowman* made me feel Christmassy inside, and I suddenly couldn't wait to join them. I rushed into the living room and gave them big hugs. My granddad had on brown trousers, a tan cable-knit cardigan over a white dress shirt, and his pointy green-and-red-striped elf cap with big fabric ears. Jim looked handsome in a red V-neck sweater and dark-grey trousers. He always acted a little uncomfortable in dressy clothes, as if he were being restricted by the fabric or something. Kailyn spun around to show off her dark-burgundy dress with a black satin sash around the waist. "I love your dress, Kiki. You look beautiful."

Without acknowledging the compliment, she asked, "Can we open gifts now?"

I laughed, reminded of why I loved celebrating Christmas with them. "Ask your dad."

"Daddy! Can we open gifts now?"

"Sure," Jim said before he popped a cheese-and-mushroom appetizer into his mouth. He picked up his wine glass off the counter and walked over to the tree to join Kailyn and me.

"Wait for me," my mom hollered from the kitchen, as she stirred the gravy on the stovetop and turned the dial to adjust the temperature. She rubbed her hands on her apron, then skipped into the living room and sat on the arm of the chair that my granddad had settled into.

Kailyn bent over to find a gift with her name on it and sat on the couch to open the wrapping. It was a gold charm bracelet from my mom. The kind you could add charms to. My mom started her off with a heart, a K, and a Hello Kitty face. I helped her put it on and then she walked across the room to give my mom a hug. "Now, open my gift for you, Colleen," Kailyn said. She grabbed a gift bag with Santa's face on it from under the tree and handed it over. My mom dug through the piles of tissue paper and pulled out a pillar candle with a glass base. "It smells like you," Kailyn declared proudly.

My mom pressed her nose to the candle and smiled. "You're right. I have a lavender-scented moisturizer that smells just like this. Thank you. It's almost too pretty to light it."

Kailyn handed each of us presents one at a time until there were only three left. One was the one from Trevor to me. I decided to wait until I saw him again to open it, so I told Kailyn to leave it under the tree. Kailyn flipped the tag on one of the last two presents and read, "To Derian from Steve."

"Oh. Did you bring this down with you?" I asked my granddad.

He nodded and seemed intrigued to know what it was. "He came by the Inn yesterday."

I unwrapped the ribbon and carefully opened the paper. It was a leather journal. "Wow. It's so nice," I said under my breath.

"This one is for you too," Kailyn shouted. "It's from Santa!"

Kailyn handed me a flat, professionally wrapped, square. The handwriting on the tag was neat. I didn't recognize it. My granddad grinned.

"I take it you brought this one down too," I said.

"Yes."

"Who's it from?"

"Santa."

"I see that. Who dropped it off at the Inn?"

He shrugged as if he'd been sworn to secrecy. "It just mysteriously appeared on the front desk this morning."

Curious, I opened it slowly. It was a vintage vinyl Ramones record.

"What is it?" my mom asked excitedly.

"A record."

"A record?" She exchanged a look with my granddad and laughed. "I didn't think kids these days knew what a record was. You don't even have a turntable."

"It's not really for playing. It's more of a collectable," I mumbled as I racked my brain trying to figure out who it could have been from. Pretty much everyone in Squamish had seen me do the Dirty Deri dance. I hoped it wasn't from a psycho stalker or something.

"Looks like you have a secret admirer," my mom said and winked. She got up and headed back into the kitchen.

Jim had an amused expression on his face. I couldn't tell if he was stoked because he liked his gifts, or because dinner was almost served, or because I got a provocative present from a secret stalker. I set the record back under the tree and went to help my mom transfer everything over to the table.

Even though we weren't at the Inn, my mom's Christmas dinner was delicious, as always. I ate way too much but still stuffed a piece of pumpkin pie down. My mom and Jim were pounding back the wine pretty good since he didn't have to drive home. At the rate the snow had piled up on the patio, I figured he might not even be able to drive home the next morning.

My granddad wrapped the leftover food to stack it in the fridge. I was washing the dishes when there was a knock at the door. My heart stretched out into twelve different directions and

114

snapped back into place. I couldn't help hoping it was Trevor. I knew the weather was too bad to make it down on the highway, and it was only seven-thirty, so he wasn't even off work yet, but I held my breath and made a wish. My mom walked to the foyer. She peeked through the peephole and stepped back to swing the door open. "Merry Christmas," she sang. "Come in, come in."

A crushing pressure hit my chest when an unfamiliar, short, thin man held up a bottle of wine and a cellophane-covered gift basket. He kissed my mom on both cheeks and greeted all of us, "Merry Christmas."

"Everyone, this is my new neighbour, Philip. Where's Simon?" She poked her head down the hall.

"Oh, he's feeling a little under the weather. He wants to rest so he'll be raring to go for our New Year's soiree, which, by the way, you are absolutely attending."

"My daughter is staying with me, so we might just have a quiet New Year's Eve at home."

"Ludicrous. You're both coming to our place. Don't even try to get out of it." He placed the gift basket on the console table in the hall and handed my mom the bottle of wine. "I don't want to interrupt your family time. And I should be getting back to Simon. He's such a baby when he's sick."

"Wait, wait. I have something for you guys." She rushed past me and opened the fridge door. She grabbed one of the tins of white-chocolate, almond, cranberry bark I had helped her make.

"Colleen, you shouldn't have, but I'm glad you did," he said when she handed him the tin. "Enjoy the rest of your evening, everyone." He waved over his shoulder as he disappeared back into the hall.

After my granddad and I finished up in the kitchen, he joined my mom and Jim in the living room. They opened another bottle of wine, laughing loudly about some old memories from Britannia that I didn't think were quite as funny as they did. At least she was less uptight when she was tipsy.

115

Kailyn dumped out the puzzle my granddad gave her and sat at the dining room table to sort the edge pieces. I sat down across from her and grouped similar colours together. It was a thousand pieces of chestnut-coloured horses running through a grassy meadow with trees in the background. Every piece was either green or brown—it was a good thing Kailyn was a whiz at puzzles because I already wanted to give up.

"I bought my mom a present," Kailyn whispered across the table.

"Really? What did you buy?"

"A red lipstick. I think she likes red lipstick."

"I'm sure she does." I glanced over at Jim. He was engrossed in a story my mom was telling.

Kailyn also glanced at her dad cautiously and lowered her voice. "Will you ask my brother for her phone number? He won't give it to me, but I know he'll give it to you."

"I don't think he'll give it to me either. He doesn't want any of us to talk to her."

"He's not the boss of us. I want to give her the lipstick."

Her expression was heart-breaking. And, although I was pretty sure it wasn't going to happen, I felt obligated to say something that would make her feel better. "I'll see what I can do. I'm not promising, though. Don't get your hopes up."

She nodded and grinned optimistically before she focused back on her puzzle. About twenty minutes later, there was another knock at the door. I didn't bother to react, because even if Trevor had gotten off work early, there was too much snow for the highway to still be open. My mom had lots of friends in the building and we'd made enough chocolate bark to fill five tins, so she was obviously expecting more drop-ins.

"Merry Christmas," she sang. "Come in, come in."

"Merry Christmas."

I recognized the voice and the puzzle piece dropped out of my hand onto the table.

CHAPTER SEVENTEEN

Trevor stood at the door and smiled in his sexy, confident trade-mark way. Literally every cell in my body felt electrified by the sight of him. It was an amazing rush. If I had known falling for him was going to feel so exhilarating, I would have done it a long time ago.

My mom gave him a hug. "I'm so glad you made it. It didn't feel quite the same without you."

Kailyn bounded across the room and wrapped her arms around his waist. He kissed the top of her head, then looked at me again.

"Hey, kid. How bad was the highway?" his dad asked.

"It's closed, but Riaz was the cop turning people around, so he let me go through. I had to use chains," he answered, without looking away from me. Then he gave me a look that made me want to run across the room and jump into his arms.

Instead, I stood up and froze like an awkward dork as he took off his boots. My mom hung his coat in the closet. He had on dark jeans and a silver-grey sweater that matched his eyes. The cold weather had made his face flushed.

After mustering the nerve, I took a deep breath and rushed over to him. I threw my arms around his neck and hugged him tightly. He loosened his embrace after what was the appropriate duration for friends. I didn't let go. When he realized I wasn't done, he squeezed me one more time and whispered, "Merry Christmas."

I tilted my head back, looked directly into his eyes, and whispered, "It is now."

Kailyn and my granddad got tired first and went to bed around midnight. My mom and Jim said good night closer to one o'clock. It had never occurred to me before, but as I watched them laugh and stumble down the hall together, I wondered if they had ever considered getting together after my dad died—not that I wanted them to. I didn't want my mom to be with anyone other than my dad, and it was hard enough to convince Trevor to not treat me like his sister. It would be impossible if I actually was his sister. "Do you think they would ever date each other?" I asked.

"No. Your mom won't set foot in Britannia. And my dad wouldn't leave it for anything."

"But do you think they're into each other?"

He shrugged as if it was obvious. "Yeah."

"That's weird."

"Weird because it's your mom and my dad, or because it's a Maverty and a Lafleur?"

"Your dad and my mom," I quickly clarified. He and I were the only other Maverty-Lafleur combination he could have been referring to, so that made me smile. "What do you think?" I ventured.

"It's weird," he agreed and stood to look more closely at the ornaments on the tree.

I sat on the couch, trying to figure out if he meant all Mavertys and Lafleurs hooking up would be weird. If I followed my mom's advice to tell him how I felt, the worst he could say was he wasn't interested and then we would just stay friends like we already were. I really had nothing to lose. Being able to force my mouth to actually say it was the only issue.

"Which ornament did you buy for your dad this year?"

"The snowflake to your right." I chuckled as I remembered my meltdown at the store. "The sales clerk thought I was seriously bent because I started bawling when I went to pay for it."

He pressed his lips together in a sympathetic way, then crouched down to pick up the present he had given me. "You haven't opened it yet."

"I wanted to wait until I saw you."

He handed it to me. "You're seeing me now."

I nodded, and my hands shook from the excitement of what could potentially happen if he had feelings for me too. "I'm really happy that I'm seeing you now, in case you couldn't tell."

He looked away and wiped the back of his hand over his mouth to hide the expression that had crept across his lips—which I assumed meant he knew exactly how I felt but wanted to avoid acknowledging it for some reason.

My face and neck heated up in what must have looked like scarlet fever. "Trevor, I—"

"Open your gift," he interrupted, as if he knew what I was going to say. He scratched the back of his neck and sat down on the couch beside me.

Not sure what I was going to say after the *Trevor, I*—anyway, I opened the wrapping. Inside, was a hand-made wooden picture frame with a photo of us when we were about seven and nine years old. I remembered the day the photo was taken because it was the first time I had reached the peak of the mountain behind Britannia. His arm was draped over my shoulder, and we were both grinning like we had conquered the world.

"I know you don't like gifts that cost a lot of money, and that's always been one of my favourite pictures of us," he explained, almost apologetically, as if he worried I wouldn't like it.

"It's adorable. Did you make the frame?"

He nodded. "I used a piece of the wood from our old tree fort. Remember when we used to have sleepovers in the tree fort?"

"Yeah, that was fun." I smiled at the memories of all our wilderness explorations together. I was always the more creative one, making him pretend we were pirates or woodland creatures. He was always the more adventurous one, making me crawl through caves or scale rock faces over waterfalls. It was such a thoughtful gift. "Thank you for making the frame, and for the photo. It reminds me of really happy times. Did you like your present?"

"I haven't opened it yet." He got up and walked over to the front hall closet. He pulled the small package out of his coat pocket and came back across the room to sit beside me. He shook it near his ear and grinned because it made a funny rattling sound. He tore open the paper and pulled out the wooden whistle I had ordered online from a vintage toy company. His initials, TJM were carved into one side of it. SAR for Search and Rescue was carved into the other side. I bit my lip and stared at him to see if he liked it. His expression was hard to read and didn't change at all as he studied the whistle in his hand.

"I know it's kind of lame, but I thought because you use a whistle for rescues it could be a funky collectable," I scrambled to explain why I thought he would like such a stupid gift.

"It's not lame, Derian. It's really cool, thanks."

He wasn't looking at me. He fidgeted with the whistle and acted as if he wanted to say something more but didn't quite know where to start. He glanced sideways at me for only a second and then stared back down at his palm. He closed his hand and made a fist around the whistle. A weird tingling sensation fluttered through my stomach like the time I had to sing for the school play.

"How's it going with Steve?" he finally asked.

It was the same question he had asked before he offered to take me to the *Footloose* play, which sent a shot of excitement through my veins. "We're just friends."

"What did he give you for Christmas?"

"A leather journal."

"What did you give him?"

Not sure why it mattered, I answered hesitantly, "A utility knife."

He looked at me again, then sighed heavily as if a weight was crushing his chest. "Who gave you that Ramones record?"

"I don't know. Someone dropped it off at the Inn. There was no name on it."

He frowned and the muscles across his shoulders tensed.

"What's wrong, Trev?"

"I have something to tell you."

"Okay," I said, cautiously optimistic. "Is it good or bad?"

He leaned his elbows on his knees and rubbed his face with his hand. "Both."

He was rattled, which was so out of character. "Just tell me."

"My dad knows a guy who runs an international Search and Rescue training facility in Iceland."

"Oh no," I breathed out, almost inaudibly.

He closed his eyes for a long blink and took a deep breath before he continued, "He arranged for Murphy and me to work there for four months. We'll be doing administration jobs, but we get to go on all the training exercises. It's an opportunity of a lifetime, and it pays better than working at the docks. It will help me save more for school."

The excitement, anxiety, and all the blood in my body felt as if they drained out of me and pooled on the floor. I saw the freaking cheese-log thing but had no clue this blow was coming. Unbelievable.

He glanced at my stunned expression and grimaced before he stared at the floor. "There's more. Murph wants to also do some travelling through Europe since we're going to be over there already. I won't have the opportunity to travel once I'm in school again." He snuck another glance, but since I still hadn't recovered from the shock, he avoided looking me directly in the eyes. "Anyway, we won't be back until summer."

"When do you leave?"

"The beginning of February."

I forced a smile in an attempt to compose myself. After some very difficult breaths I was able to say, "It sounds like an amazing opportunity. I'm really happy for you."

Reading through my effort to be positive, he leaned over, wrapped his arm across my shoulder, and pulled my body against him. "You probably won't even miss me. You'll be busy studying, dating, going to parties, and having fun." He tightened the hug until I could feel his heartbeat, steady and strong. "You'll be fine without me."

"Fine" was a relative term. I would survive, but that didn't mean it was what I wanted. Accepting we would never be romantically involved was hard enough. Having to come to terms with him not being in my life at all was going to suck. "I'm going to miss you so much."

"I'm going to miss you, too." After a long silence, he kissed the top of my head and said, "It's getting late. You should go to bed. I'll crash on the couch."

"I want to stay here with you." My heart jumped from the shock of saying something so impulsive.

Although it appeared he considered it for a second, he shook his head. "We can talk about everything more tomorrow."

There weren't going to be any more opportunities to tell him how I felt, and I didn't have anything to lose. If it went horribly, he would leave and hopefully forget about it. If he felt the same way, we could maybe get together when he came back. Either way, I needed to say it so I would have no regrets. I took a deep breath and prepared to do the most terrifying thing I had ever done. "Trevor, I—"

As if he had anticipated what I was going to blurt out, he pressed his fingertip against my lips with the gentlest touch and whispered, "Shh. Don't."

"But I—" I struggled to speak without being able to move my lips.

"Please don't, Deri." He closed his eyes for a long blink, then leaned forward and kissed my cheek. "Good night."

Completely confused, I stood and rushed down the hall to my room. I turned on the bedside lamp and checked to see if the light was going to wake Kailyn. She was out cold, so I slid my phone off my desk and texted Sophie: *Trevor showed up! Drove down in a snow storm. For me? Seemed that way. Everything awesome. All alone. Drops a bomb. Going to work at SAR facility in Iceland then party around Europe w/ Murph until summer. Tried to tell him how I feel about him. Stopped me, said 'please don't'. Told me to go to bed. WTF?*

Kailyn was sprawled across my entire bed, but it didn't matter because I didn't anticipate falling asleep. It took a few minutes before my phone buzzed loudly with the response from Sophie: *WTF? is right. Call me.*

Can't. Kailyn is in my room.

k. How did he know ur going to spill it?

I was so obvious. He didn't want to hear me say it. Why?

Dating someone else?

Id think so. Maybe saving me the humiliation b/c he doesn't feel the same way? Maybe wants someone with more experience? Maybe wants to sleep his way through every woman in Europe?

Maybe too hard to leave for Europe if he actually heard u say it.

That one struck me because it was a possibility that had never occurred to me. *Oh. U think?*

Ya.

Either way, I'm going to miss him so much.

I know. Call me in the am so we can talk. xoxo

k. thanks.

I put the phone down and sat on the edge of my bed for a while, contemplating my options. Give up, bury my feelings and let him go live his life without me. Or, spend some quality time with him before I bury my feelings and let him go live his life without me. It was possibly my last opportunity to be close to him, so I chose option two, psyched myself up, and tip-toed down the hall into the living room. He had unplugged the Christmas tree lights, but the light coming in through the windows was bright enough to see that he was stretched out on the couch, awake. His stare was intense and made my heart pound in my throat. "You okay?" he asked.

"Um." I tucked my hair behind my ears, hoping for the courage I needed. "I can't sleep. Would it be all right if we pretend we're in the tree house?"

After a pause that made my legs weak, he lifted the blanket without saying anything. Relieved, I slid in beside him and nestled into his arms as they wrapped around me. His breath slowed and the rhythm made me relax. The feel of his body against mine was like a dream come true, even if it was only for one night. I decided there was no point telling him my true feelings if he was leaving for half a year. Everything could change in that amount of time. All I wanted to do was enjoy the time we did have. I was almost asleep when he sighed. I was a little drowsy, but it sounded like he mumbled, "Shit."

CHAPTER EIGHTEEN

I hardly saw Trevor for the month before he left. He worked double shifts at the docks, stopped coming over for breakfast, and spent all of his free time either going on rescues or doing errands with Murphy to get ready for their trip. Although he would have flipped out if I ever compared him to his mom to his face, taking off and avoiding conversations was his way of dealing with a lot of things—just like her. It's why he hiked, why he bought a motorbike, and why he travelled so much. The only difference between Trevor and his mom was he always came back. At least, he always had in the past.

As a result of his master evasion techniques, we never got a chance to talk about what it meant that we fell asleep together on the couch at Christmas. Boxing Day morning, I had slipped back into my room before anyone woke up. By the time I got up for breakfast, he had already left. His dad said he had to work, but I knew he took off to avoid me. It was pretty obvious he was going to continue dodging me until he got on the airplane. I was bummed, and Sophie was sick of my crappy mood.

"Trevor leaves tomorrow," I moaned and thudded my head down on the table in the students' lounge.

"Good," Sophie snorted. "Will you please stop moping once he's gone?"

"I'll probably only get worse," I mumbled into the wood of the table.

"I'll do an intervention if you don't watch it."

"I wanna be sedated."

"That's it!"

"What?" I sat up and glared at her. "I was joking. I'm not going to take sedatives."

"No, we need to party."

My posture collapsed again as I sunk into the chair, depressed. "I don't feel like partying."

"I know. That's why we're going to. Doug, party at your house Saturday night?"

"Yup."

"There you go." She raised her eyebrows and flashed her calculated grin. "I'll be right back. I'm going to throw a few invites around." She stood and walked towards Steve and his friends before I even had a chance to protest.

Steve and I hadn't talked about that date he asked me on before Christmas because his sister had to be hospitalized again with complications. He was too preoccupied. I was too mopey. Sophie sat down at a free chair at Steve's table and talked with erratic hand gestures. He looked over at me and smiled, so I waved. He got up when Sophie did and they walked in opposite directions. He walked towards me. She walked towards the table where Mason was sitting. Paige Peterson had just plopped herself down to sit sideways on Mason's lap and leaned in to kiss his neck. Obviously, the PDA didn't deter Sophie. She walked right up to them. Mason moved Paige off his lap, which made her pout and walk away.

"Hey," Steve said as he sat down next to me.

"Hey. How's your sister doing?"

"About the same. Her liver and kidneys aren't functioning

properly still. They decided to keep her in the hospital because she keeps getting blood clots from the medications they have her on. Sorry I've been kind of MIA."

"It's totally fine. How are you doing?"

"I don't know." He shrugged, and the expression that flashed across his face made him look old. "Giselle is all anybody in my family talks about. Sometimes I want to laugh at something funny one of my friends said, or something I saw on TV, and then I remember my sister's in the hospital and I feel guilty for being happy."

"You're allowed to feel happy. It doesn't mean you don't care about what she's going through. It just means you're human and you want to feel better."

"I guess." He sighed and looked at the wall. "I feel like I can't think straight. I'm tired all day, but then at night when I go to bed, I can't sleep."

"I haven't been sleeping all that well lately either."

"Right. You're sad because Trevor's leaving."

It was true, and obvious to anyone around me that I was distraught, but for some reason I didn't appreciate him pointing it out. "I'm allowed to be upset that one of my best friends is leaving."

Doug looked up from the Dostoyevsky book he was reading, interested in the conversation at the table for once.

"I didn't say you couldn't be upset." Steve said cautiously, as if he could tell I was on the brink of a meltdown. "I understand that you and Trevor are close, and you're going to miss him." He glanced over at Doug, who was still watching in hopes of a blowout.

"Sorry," I mumbled, wishing I hadn't been so defensive. It wasn't Steve's fault that things didn't work out between Trevor and me.

Sophie returned and said, "Well, it looks like everybody in the school is going to be there. Is that cool, Doug?"

"Yup." He buried his nose back in the book, no longer interested if I wasn't going to lose it on Steve.

"Everyone in the school?" I asked and looked over my shoulder at Mason. Paige was saddled up on him again.

"Would you like to go to the party with me, Derian?" Steve asked.

I bit at my lip and thought about Trevor. It was disappointing to admit, but dating Trevor had been a pipe dream. It was beyond me what made me believe he might want to date a young, inexperienced, naïve girl when he had the opportunity to have epic flings with multiple sophisticated women in Europe and then university once he was back. I needed to move on with my life, and probably the sooner the better if I wanted to get over it. Getting some dating experience with a thoughtful, intelligent, good-looking guy like Steve was definitely not a bad consolation, so I said, "Sure."

"Great." Steve stood. "I have to go do some catch-up work in the biology lab right now. I'll pick you up at the Inn around eight on Saturday night."

"Do you want help with your lab?"

"Sure." He held out his arm to hold my hand. I stood and somewhat awkwardly took his hand.

Sophie flashed a peace sign and a huge satisfied grin.

Trevor had to leave for the airport at four o'clock on Saturday morning. He didn't come over to say goodbye on Friday night like I had expected him to, so I woke myself up at three-thirty with my alarm. I layered my winter parka over my pyjamas and sat on the porch railing to wait.

The outside light to his house flicked on at about three-forty-five, and his dad stepped out with Trevor's duffle bag. He threw it into the back of his Ford F350, then he went back into the house. The light from their living room angled out the open front door and made a warm glow on the porch. Jim appeared again and walked over to get in the truck and start the engine. I jumped

128

down from the railing and clomped across the parking lot in my snowmobile boots. Trevor saw me as soon as he stepped through the doorway. His muscles tensed before he shut the door behind him. We stood staring at each other in silence.

Eventually, I spoke. "You weren't going to leave without saying goodbye, were you?"

His resolve to steer clear of me melted away. He took long strides forward, dropped his backpack on the ground, wrapped his arms around me, and lifted me off the ground. I pressed the side of my face against his neck and held him so tightly it was probably strangling him. After he put me down, he rested his forehead on mine.

I wanted to get mad at him for being like his mom and trying to take off without a word, but I couldn't bear the thought of us being on bad terms. "Be safe, Trev."

"Always am," he choked out. He cupped his hands on either side of my face and ran his thumbs over my cheeks to wipe away my tears. His weight shifted forward, but instead of kissing me, as I hoped, he gently touched the tip of his nose to the tip of my nose. He inhaled deeply as if what he was about to do required a ton of strength. His hands slipped away from my face, he picked up his backpack and got into his dad's truck. I had to move so they could back up. Trevor didn't look at me as they drove away.

Once I was back inside the Inn, I didn't bother to take my boots or parka off before I got into bed. I was too sad to even cry.

When I finally dragged myself out of bed, I almost called Steve to cancel our date. I didn't because I decided it would be easier to distract myself if I went to the party. He showed up at the Inn with a bouquet of Gerber daisies, which was sweet. Before we headed out to Doug's house, I made him promise we wouldn't talk about the things that were making us sad. He shook my hand to seal the deal.

The party was insane. Sophie wasn't kidding when she said the entire school was going to show up. Doug's parents were both partiers, so they didn't care as long as the cops didn't get called, and as long as nobody drove if they'd been drinking. Ironically, the band didn't usually play at their own parties, so the music blasted from a stereo system instead.

"Do you want to dance?" Steve asked over the noise. He looked good in dark jeans and a retro Aerosmith concert T-shirt.

"Sure."

He led me out to the dance floor and he kept glancing at my body as we danced. Even though the song was fast, he pulled me close and we moved more like we were dirty dancing. I didn't mind. It felt good to know he liked me in that way.

As we did a slow grind, images flicked through my mind.

A forest and deep snow. A small blonde girl in a red jacket huddled under a tree, hugging her knees into her chest. A chocolate-brown lab snuggled up close to her.

"Derian." Steve squeezed my arm. "Deri. Are you okay?"

I smiled to cover it up and took a deep breath. "Yeah, I zoned out for a second. Sorry."

"Do you have epilepsy?"

"No. I'm fine. Really." The girl in the vision wasn't familiar to me. I tried to see more, but nothing came to me. It was so frustrating to only have bits and pieces to work with. The music was too loud to focus, so I pulled Steve's hand and led him down the hall towards the den.

"Where are you taking me?" he asked with a suggestive lift of his eyebrows.

I shoved his shoulder playfully. "You're not getting lucky, if that's what you're hoping."

"Well, if you don't want to tell me why you looked like you were having some sort of seizure, you're going to have to distract me with a little action." He winked.

I turned and leaned my back against the wall. He smiled and

rested his arm on the wall above me. He was acting sexy. I grabbed his shirt and tugged it lightly to pull his body towards mine. "It wasn't a seizure." I wanted to kiss him. I didn't kiss him, though, because I was pretty sure missing Trevor was the only reason I felt the urge.

"If it wasn't a seizure, what was it? You didn't take drugs, did you?"

"No."

He stepped back to study my eyes for signs that I had taken something.

"You promised we wouldn't talk about anything that makes us sad. Remember?"

He stared at me as if he wasn't sure whether to let it go or not. A party was not the best place to focus on developing my intuition anyway, so I ran my hands up his abs and over his chest. Partly because I was trying to distract him and partly because I wondered what it would feel like. He smiled in a slightly confused way. "Are you putting the moves on me, Miss Lafleur?"

I wrapped my arms around his neck, stood on my tiptoes, and kissed his ear. "I'm just trying to distract—"

He abruptly stepped forward and pushed me against the wall. I couldn't finish my sentence because he kissed me hard. His hands ran over my hip and up the sides of my body. His thumb grazed the side of my chest purposefully, but he was cool about it and kept moving up towards my neck. His hands were warm as he moved them over the curves of my body. He leaned his weight closer to me, and I could feel his heart beating against my chest. I didn't know if it was because I was depressed, or because Steve was a really good kisser, but what he was doing was hot and I didn't want him to stop.

After we kissed for a while, he breathed into my ear, "You are so beautiful. Good job at distracting me."

I laughed. "Maybe we should dance again."

"Or we could find a private place and you could distract me

some more." He kissed his way along my jaw and down my neck.

I shook my head, not ready for anything quite that ambitious.

He stopped but didn't lean back. It seemed as if he really wanted to keep kissing me. Eventually, he shifted his weight and stood up tall. "I'm not the one you want to be kissing, am I?"

It took me a while to fumble through excuses in my mind. "I, um, that's not it." I tucked my hair behind my ears and stared at his chest. "It's kind of embarrassing to admit, but I'm really inexperienced in the boy department. I'm not ready yet."

Without even trying to change my mind, he nodded and said, "All right, let's dance." He held my hand to head back towards the living room. We approached Mason, who stood with his back against the wall, waiting for the bathroom.

Steve pulled me closer and acknowledged him, "Cartwright."

"Hey."

We squeezed past him. I glanced over my shoulder. He smiled when our eyes met. God. He was devastatingly handsome.

CHAPTER NINETEEN

There was something about the way Mason smiled at me that I couldn't wipe from my mind. It reminded me of how, right before Giselle had collapsed, he had crossed the room as if he maybe planned to talk to me. Also, I never forgot the way he had hesitated when he saw me crying in the hall. He seemed sweet. It made me wonder if he did know who I was, and maybe would be interested in getting to know me even better. Who knew? Sophie told me not to sell myself short. I scanned the room and when I spotted Sophie, I turned to Steve. "Do you mind getting us something to drink?"

"Your wish is my command. I'll be right back."

Sophie and Doug were making out on the couch, so I sat on the armchair and stared at them until they felt my presence. Sophie lifted her head and sat up, straddled over Doug's thighs. "Sorry to interrupt."

"Sure you are." Sophie feigned a snarl.

"Yeah, you're right, I don't care. You guys have plenty of time to do that."

"This better be good," she said as she reached over to grab her red plastic cup off the coffee table.

"I think so. Close your ears, Doug."

"Okay," he said, but he didn't cover his ears.

"So, I have very strong feelings for Trevor, as you know, but Trevor just took off and is going to be gone for almost half a year. I'm very unclear on the status of our relationship because it's not technically something we've ever talked about. So, if I think out loud here, he kinda, sorta asked me on one date that we never went on, and we kinda sorta slept together, but we had our clothes on, and although I've sat on his lap in my underwear, we've never even kissed on the lips. Presumably, one of the reasons nothing happened between us is because he prefers mature, sexually confident women, not reserved girls who are too wimpy to even talk about a relationship, let alone have one. So, long story short, I assume it's a good idea for me to get as much experience as possible while he's gone."

"Yes," they both said in unison.

"Okay, well, in that case. At the risk of sounding sleazy, would it be out of the question to date more than one person at a time?"

"Ooh," Sophie squealed. "Who?"

Doug frowned.

"I was thinking maybe Mason."

"No." Doug shook his head adamantly.

"What do you mean no? Why?" Sophie asked.

"Unless she's looking for a one-night stand, Cartwright's not the guy for Deri." He shot me a cautionary look. "And I'll tell you right now, Trevor will lose his shit on Mason if he uses you."

"Trevor's not here," I reminded him.

"Doesn't matter. He. Will. Lose. His. Shit."

"It's really none of his business. I can do whatever I choose, thanks."

Doug sat up and shot me a serious look. "Listen, Deri, I think it's cool that you're trying to come out of your shell and experiment a bit, but you don't need to go crazy. You can date Steve but not Mason."

Sophie shoved his chest. "Why are you acting like a control freak? Deri can date both of them if she wants to."

"Mason is just going to sleep with her and leave her. Trevor asked me to keep an eye on her, and he wouldn't be cool with that."

"What?" I blinked repeatedly as what he said sunk in. "You and Trevor talked about me before he left? What else did he say?"

Sophie spun around and waited for Doug to answer. Doug didn't answer exactly, he shrugged as if he regretted the disclosure.

"What else did he say?" I repeated.

"He just asked me to keep an eye on you."

My eyebrows angled into a frown as I attempted to interpret what that implied. "The protective way you would keep an eye on his kid sister for him, or the possessive way you would keep an eye on a potential girlfriend to make sure no one moves in on her?"

Doug took too long to answer, so Sophie punched his arm. "What was it—kid sister or girlfriend?"

"Ow! I don't know why Trevor is all hyper-protective over Derian."

"Has he said he likes her?"

"We're not girls," Doug protested. "We don't talk about shit like that. All I know is that Trevor will mess up anybody who hurts you. I don't know if it's because he cares about you like a sister, a girlfriend, or both."

My head spun with what it all meant, so I clarified, "And who decided I have permission to date Steve, you or Trevor?"

He shook his head, obviously wishing he'd never promised Trevor he would take care of it. "Just stay away from Mason."

"Thanks for your concern, but I think I'll make my own decisions from here on in." I stood and pointed at them with authority. "As you were."

Doug looked uneasy. Sophie looked amused by the drama my more assertive self had stirred up. She pulled Doug in and continued their make-out session where it left off. I turned around and looked for Steve. He was talking to Lisa Alvarez, so I stood next to him. He turned when he noticed me, and kissed my cheek before handing me a bottle of water. Lisa smiled coldly and walked away.

"Are you going to tell me what was going on with you earlier?" he asked.

I squished up my face. "I thought I distracted you enough to forget about that."

"I've recovered."

I sighed and debated whether to tell him about the intuition. Only my family, Trevor's family, and Sophie knew I could do it. It hadn't been happening all that much, so I decided to lie and not weird him out. "I get mini migraines. They don't last long. The doctor says they're nothing to be concerned about. Should we dance again?"

I tugged his hand and led him back out onto the dance floor to end the conversation. He didn't seem to mind. When the song was over, I looked across the room at Mason. He was surrounded by a harem. A competition I had no business entering. What made me think I could date a guy like Mason, let alone Mason and Steve at the same time? It was conceited and selfish to have even considered it. When did I become that girl? Maybe it was time to go back to sweet, bookish Derian and abandon high-on-herself, boy-obsessed Derian.

CHAPTER TWENTY

The vision of the little girl in the snow didn't happen again, but I searched the face of every kid I saw in town and at the Inn, hoping to recognize her or her dog. I also scoured the news to check if any children were missing. Nothing came of all my vigilance, so I tried to put it out of my mind.

Although I had decided that attempting to date two guys in order to shape myself into a viable contender for Trevor's affections was arrogant and ridiculous, I was still irritated with Doug for telling me what I could and couldn't do. It was bad enough when Trevor acted like my big brother. I didn't need Doug doing it too. He thought it was funny I was giving him the silent treatment, and his smug expression is what finally made me break my stand-off. We were sitting at our table in the students' lounge. "Wipe that satisfied look off your face."

"Why? I did a good deed. I saved you from being used by a womanizer."

"Isn't that a little judgy? You don't even know him."

"Neither do you."

"Well, I'm free to get to know him if I want to." I glared at Doug with the most defiant look I could muster.

"Go ahead. You'll just find out that I'm right. In the process, you'll lose what you have with Steve. If you want to learn about the shitty side of dating the hard way, suit yourself. I'm just trying to save you the heartache. And the potential unwanted pregnancy."

I shook my head, pissed that he didn't trust my judgment. I was still squinting, and he was still smiling as Sophie walked up and sat between us. "Aw, so cute, look at my two besties getting along so nicely."

"Doug feels I'm too naïve to make my own decisions, so I'm going to become friends with Mason, just to spite him." I stuck my tongue out at him, then ate a spoonful of my pasta.

Doug laughed. "All right, but when it all blows up in your face I'm going to sit here and tell you *I told you so*."

"Whatever. I can't waste any more time on boys, anyway. My GPA is suffering. I need to get some homework finished." I stood and packed my things into my bag. "I'll see you guys later." I left the lounge and something crashed against a locker down the hall. Then I heard Nikolai's cartoony voice say, "Stop". I rushed towards the art wing, where the noise had come from.

"Hey! Cut it out." A male voice intervened before I got there.

Once I rounded the corner, I saw Nikolai sprawled out on the floor, reaching for his glasses. He tried to put them on, but the frame was twisted, and one of the lenses had a big crack across it. He was surrounded by a crowd of grade-eight and nine boys, and Mason.

"Don't mess with him again or you'll be laid out on the floor," Mason said, which made the boys all scatter. "You okay, Niko?"

Nikolai nodded, but he didn't look okay. I stepped around Mason and sat down on the floor beside Nikolai. "What happened?"

Mason leaned against the locker to listen to the answer.

Nikolai shrugged. "Same as always. They tease me because I'm small and because of my voice."

"Your voice?" I reached over and rested my hand on his

forearm. "I love your voice. It makes me happy."

His face turned red and his big brown eyes filled up with tears. "My voice is embarrassing. I went to a speech doctor when I was little, but it didn't help. I hate how it sounds."

"I don't agree. It's unique and original. Sometimes people don't understand how cool something is if it's a one-of-a-kind." I picked up his glasses and tried to straighten out the frame. "You should be proud of all the things that make you special and interesting." I considered telling him about my brain glitch but didn't want Mason to hear. Maybe I needed to take my own advice before telling other people what to do.

"Were you ever teased?" Nikolai asked.

"Yeah. The kids in elementary school used to tease me because of my name. They would come up with a different dairy product every week to call me—cheddar, Gouda, skim, two percent, sour cream. Kefir was one of the more creative ones. Even the teacher accidentally called me that one."

Nikolai laughed, then pointed at Mason. "That's Mason. He tutors me in science. Mason, this is my big buddy, Derian."

Mason extended his arm to shake my hand and said, "Nice to officially meet you."

"You too." That was all I could manage to say to him because I suddenly felt insanely nervous in his presence. Instead, I turned back to Nikolai. "I'll make you a deal. If you try to be proud of the things that make you different from everyone else, I will too."

"Okay."

I stood and helped Nikolai to his feet. "If they bother you again, let me know. I'll ask Doug to talk to them."

He raised one eyebrow and said, "They'd be more afraid of Sophie."

The fact that he was dead serious made me laugh. She could be very intimidating if she wanted to be. "Okay. I'll ask Sophie to take care of it if they ever bother you again." I glanced at Mason, wishing I had the nerve to strike up a conversation with him. "I should get going. I'll see you around, Nikolai. Don't forget to be proud of what makes you unique."

"You too." He pointed at me. They both smiled, and my cheeks flushed as I walked away.

I headed to the computer room. With everything that had been going on for me emotionally, I had gotten behind on a few assignments, which was so unlike me. I hadn't even fallen behind the year after my dad died. The fact that a bit of boy drama threw me off wasn't something I was particularly proud of. So, with renewed determination to be a serious and focused student, I got to work.

After I typed an essay for English, I checked my email, fingers crossed, hoping Trevor had sent a reply to my message. So much for avoiding distractions.

My inbox was empty, which should have cemented my resolve to focus only on academics, but it actually made me think about Trevor more. What the hell was wrong with me?

Corrine Andrews leaned over from the computer station next to mine. "Sounds like your brother is having a wicked time."

"What?"

"I would have been scared shitless if I was with Murphy when he ran into that polar bear."

Polar bear? Brother? Corrine Andrews speaking to me? "Trevor's been emailing you? I didn't know you guys were friends."

She chuckled in a stuck-up way. "I guess we're not the kind of friends brothers tell their sisters about."

"Trevor and I aren't related."

"You're not?"

"No. Excuse me." I rushed out of the computer room, got my stuff out of my locker, and kept going right out of the school. Steve was out front, throwing a football around with some of his friends.

"Hey, Deri," he hollered.

I didn't feel like talking, so I turned in the opposite direction,

140

wrapped my arms around my body, and walked with my head down.

"Derian. Wait up." I could hear him running after me, and I seriously considered breaking into a sprint to avoid him. He was going to chat my ear off as usual, and all I really wanted was to be left alone in peace and quiet. "Hey." He pulled at my elbow to make me turn around. "What's wrong?"

"I'm having a bad day."

He draped his arm over my shoulder and walked with me.

"You don't have a coat on. You're going to freeze," I pointed out.

"Nah, I'm a warm guy. So, are we ditching our afternoon classes?"

"I am."

"Then I am too. I have an idea, if you're interested."

I really wanted to be alone, but it wasn't fair to take my bad mood out on him when he was just trying to be friendly. He had enough to worry about without having to deal with me blowing him off too. "What is it?"

"You'll see."

We walked for twenty minutes to a strip mall. He was freezing, I could tell. He didn't complain, though. He led me down a wide set of stairs towards the bowling alley under the strip mall. It bustled with seniors, who looked pretty serious about their bowling. The noise of balls hitting the hardwood and the tumbling pins filled the air as we rented shoes and chose balls. I hadn't been bowling since I was about twelve. It felt a little weird to be in the same alley that my dad used to take me to. It looked and smelled exactly the same.

"Do you come here a lot?" I asked.

"Only when the girl I like is walking away from school in the middle of the day, looking sad. Do you come here a lot?"

"Only when I'm walking away from school in the middle of the day, feeling sad, and the guy who likes me follows me."

His jaw tensed for a second, then he covered it up with a forced smile. It took a second to occur to me that his reaction was because I said he was the guy who liked me and not the guy who I liked.

"You're up first," he said as he handed me my ball.

We bowled for two hours. It was really fun. Afterwards, we sat at the diner counter to share an order of fries. I picked the stool my dad sat on. It made me sad to think about how those memories would slip farther and farther into the past, with no new memories to replace them.

Steve must have noticed how I was feeling. He asked, "Did you used to come here with your dad?"

I nodded and held back the emotion that built in my throat.

"I was trying to cheer you up. We can leave if it makes you sad."

"It's okay. I like remembering. I just wish I had more things to remember." I dipped a fry in the ketchup, but didn't eat it.

"The Inn must be exactly the way it was then."

"For the most part, but my granddad is trying to sell it. If a developer buys it, all those memories will be lost forever."

Steve nodded and ate a fry. "Maybe he'll change his mind."

"I doubt it. He's getting older. Plus, once I leave for university, he'll have the extra expense of hiring someone to replace me. It would be better for him if he retired to go play golf somewhere. But it breaks my heart to think the memories of my childhood and my dad will be gone forever."

"My grandpa retired for two months, then went back to work part-time because he missed the routine and the people. Your family has lived in Britannia Beach for three generations. If there is a way financially for your grandpa to keep the place I'm sure he would rather do that. I doubt he wants to move to Florida or Palm Springs by himself."

I looked at him and smiled because that did sound somewhat reassuring. He stole a sip of my lemonade. Then we talked about his sister and the complications she was still dealing with until a bunch of young kids came in and it got noisy. As we were leaving, I said, "Thanks. I feel way better."

He stopped on the stairs and eased me against the wall to kiss me. His body felt warm against mine. I was kind of into it until he unzipped my coat and slid his hands up from my waist and under my sweater towards my chest. I pulled back abruptly and zipped my coat back up.

He smiled with only half his mouth. It looked like he was both disappointed and a little bit irritated at the same time. He didn't say anything about it, though. He held out his hand, wrapped his fingers around mine, and we walked back to the school. I waited in his truck as he went to his locker to get his stuff. It was hard to tell if I was really not into Steve in a physical way, or if I was just really, really bad at the whole dating thing, or if I was hung up on the hope of dating Trevor when he got back. I still hadn't decided which one it was when Steve climbed into the truck and drove me home.

He parked in front of the Inn and I said, "I'm sorry I'm an emotional roller coaster. I don't mean to lead you on or be a tease. I'm just a total newbie with all this, and I keep doing everything wrong. You must think I'm so difficult."

He chuckled. "You're a little complicated, but that's one of the things I like about you."

"Would it be okay if I asked you to take it slow with the physical side of our relationship and be patient while I sort things out personally?"

"Sure, I can wait as long as you want to. Would you like to go out for dinner on Saturday night?"

"Yes." I leaned over and kissed him. "Thanks for understanding, and thanks for the bowling, and thanks for the talk, and thanks for the ride home."

"You're welcome. If you want to ditch again tomorrow, I know of a cheap movie theatre that plays horrors in the afternoon."

I tapped his shoulder with the back of my hand. "I think you've missed enough school this year, young man. I'll try to be a better influence on you."

"I wouldn't mind if you were a little naughty some of the time." He angled his eyebrows in a sassy way.

"I bet." I smiled and shook my head. "Bye."

CHAPTER TWENTY-ONE

After Steve dropped me off, I went to my bedroom and turned on my laptop. I finally had an email from Trevor in my inbox.

Hey Deri, sorry I haven't written you back since I got here. I wish you were here so badly right now. I had a really shitty day today. It was the worst call I've ever been on. We were asked to join a search after a local SAR had already looked for a day. We helped for another two days, but we had to call it off because of bad weather. She probably won't make it another night. I've never failed in a search before. It's such a helpless feeling. The part that kills me the most is she's only five years old. Remember when Giselle got hurt, you said you didn't like emergencies because you felt like you couldn't help? Now I know what you meant. It sucks. If you were here, I would say thanks for listening and I would need a hug. I miss you so much. Trev

I read his message three times, then wrote back:

Did the little girl have blonde hair? Was she wearing a red jacket? Was she with a chocolate-brown lab? I had a vision like that. I would have told you if I knew it was linked to you. Maybe she'll make it through another night. It will be so sad if she doesn't, but it's not your fault. I know you did your best. You always do. Even though we're far apart I will always be here for you to talk to. I'm sending you a hug with my mind. I hope you can feel it. I miss you

145

more than words could ever describe. Tell Murphy it's not his fault either. I know you both did everything possible. D.

My feelings were mixed—ecstatic that he chose to reach out to me when it was something important, but horrible that it was because they couldn't find the little girl and that she was probably going to die.

Before I went to bed, I wrote in the journal Steve gave me. I hoped that putting everything out on paper would maybe produce some clues or trigger the vision again. Forty-five minutes of writing later, I was frustrated. And exhausted. So, I went to sleep.

My phone rang and woke me up when it was pitch black in my room. Groggy, I had to blink a couple of times to make the numbers on the display less fuzzy. It was three in the morning. "Hello," I croaked.

"Hey, Deri," Trevor whispered. "Sorry to wake you. I need you to think for a second. The girl you saw in your vision is the girl we're looking for. She has blonde hair, she was wearing a red jacket, and her dog is with her. Did you see anything else in the environment that might help us figure out where she is?"

I rubbed my eyes and tried to wake myself up. "Um, it was snowing, and she was huddled in the well of a tree with the dog." As I said it, an image of a waterfall flashed in my mind. "Are there twin falls near the search area?"

"Yes." He sounded stoked.

"She's near there."

"Thanks, Deri." It sounded as if he stood abruptly, followed by rushed shuffling in the background as if people were on the move. "You're awesome. You can go back to sleep now."

"Okay. I love you." I hung up and when I realized what had come out of my mouth, I sat up in my bed—fully awake.

I texted Sophie in the morning to tell her I needed an emergency consultation as soon as she got to school. Mornings were not her

146

thing, but she dragged her ass in early because I typed 911 at the end of my text. "This better be good, or really bad," she moaned and leaned against my locker.

"I don't even know where to start. Okay, so after lunch yesterday, I found my little grade-eight buddy getting beat up by a bunch of boys and guess who was saving him?" I waited for her to guess, but it was too early. She just shook her head to refuse the effort. "Mason. Mason was saving him. It turns out he also tutors my little buddy in science, and did I tell you that he volunteered for the food drive before Christmas? Anyway, I think he might be a better guy than Doug thinks he is. Not the point, though." I told her everything that happened after that, Corrine, bowling, and making out on the stairs with Steve.

"Wow. Stevie Rawlings with the moves. Was it clumsy?"

"No. He knows what he's doing."

"Mmm. Tell me more."

"There is no more. I basically jumped away and told him I wanted to take things slow. Do you think my problem is me, Steve, or Trevor?"

"If Trevor tried to get up in your business would you let him?"

"I would let him do way more than that."

"Easy there." She laughed. "The problem is you."

"Yeah, well, I guess I already knew that. So anyway, Trevor wrote to me because he had a really bad call, and he was upset. I wrote back and told him I had a vision with a little girl, wondering if it was the same girl they'd been looking for."

Sophie opened her mouth as if she were going to ask a question. I held up my hand to stop her.

"So then, Trevor called from Iceland wanting to know what else I saw in the vision. He was excited by the lead and thanked me. Then I said..." I paused dramatically and smiled because I knew Sophie was going to go berserk when I told her.

"Oh my God, what did you say?"

"I said I love you without even thinking. It just slipped out right before I hung up."

"Awesome." She clapped as she hopped up and down on the spot. "This was totally worth getting up early for. You're the best best-friend ever."

"What's got her all excited this early in the morning?" Doug asked as he joined us.

"Oh, so you think I'm talking to you now?" I joked.

"You better be. I just signed up to send you a flower for Valentine's Day."

"Oh, so sweet. Okay, I forgive you. Sophie's excited because I have a pathetic love life and it amuses her."

Doug leaned over and kissed her neck. "I like when she's amused. Thanks Deri."

"Our sweet little Derian finally said the L word to a boy," Sophie crooned as she pinched my cheek. "The next step is to get her to make the L word to a boy."

"Okay, that's enough mocking for one day. Bu-bye."

"Wait." Sophie pouted over Doug's shoulder. "We have more gossiping to do."

"School first. Drama second. I need to graduate with a stellar GPA."

Sophie laughed. "You could drop out now and still end up with a better GPA than mine."

"Regardless, all of our feminist ancestors are currently rolling their eyes at me for letting my attempts to acquire a love life take priority over academics."

Sophie shrugged as if she didn't agree. "Those goals aren't mutually exclusive. You can be a strong, independent, educated woman and engage in intimate relationships at the same. Kiss a boy and cure cancer. Kiss a girl and fly on a mission to Neptune. Get a vibrator and design the next Taj Mahal. Or, pine over Trevor in Iceland and ace high school. You can do it all."

"See." I pointed at Doug. "You can't tell me what to do. I can

148

date whomever I want and be whomever I want to be; however, who I want to be right now is an eleventh-grade graduate. I'll see you guys later. Bye."

CHAPTER TWENTY-TWO

On February 14th, I sent Trevor an animated e-card and asked for an update on the search. At school, I got single roses from Doug, Steve, Nikolai, and a Secret Admirer. I'd made cupcakes at the Inn the night before and iced them with thick pink icing. I gave one to Kailyn, one to Jim, and one to my granddad before I left for school. Sophie, Doug, Steve, and Nikolai each got one. And I ate one myself. That left one, and I wanted to give it to Mason. But I hadn't seen him all day.

After school, I finally spotted him at his locker. I was literally two feet away and about to hand him the cupcake when he closed his locker, turned in the opposite direction, and disappeared into the crowd of students.

"Hey, is that an extra cupcake?" Steve asked as he wrapped his arms around my waist from behind. I held it up so he could take a bite. A clump of icing stuck to his lip. He looked really cute, so I licked the icing off, which he definitely liked. "I've got something for you." He placed a small pink-and-red-striped box on my palm. His eyebrows rose in an encouraging way, so I opened it and found a pair of gold heart earrings.

"Thanks." I tilted my face up and kissed him. "They're cute."

"There's more." He handed me a scrapbook with a black-and-white photo of the Inn on the front. He grinned, excited to give it to me. "Open it."

I lifted the cover and flipped through the pages slowly, examining each of the photographs in detail. He'd taken art-style photos of historical details of the Inn. The first was a close-up of the light-blue paint chipping off the wood window frame. He captured the mountain in the reflection of the window. It was amazing. There were also shots of the chrome that edged the kitchen counter; the original hardwood planks in the library; the tiles around the fireplace; the glass door knob of one of the guest rooms; the hand-painted, wood Britannia Beach sign; the old rowboat we used as kids; and a wide shot of my parents' room.

My mom had donated my dad's clothes about two months after he died, but we didn't change anything else in their room. It was exactly the same as the day he died. The maids cleaned it, and sometimes I sat in the window seat to read, but other than that, nobody ever went into it. I flipped back to the beginning of the scrapbook and looked at each photo again.

"Do you like it?" he asked softly.

I nodded, fighting back tears, and hugged him.

When I released his neck, he stepped back and looked directly into my eyes. "Derian, would you like to be my girlfriend?"

Whoa. Wow. I probably blinked ten times before I could even start to form thoughts. Sophie's comment about having the freedom to pursue personal goals and romantic goals at the same time had actually convinced me I wasn't completely wasting my life just because I was interested in the opposite sex. Trevor was going to be away until the summer, Mason barely knew I existed, and Steve was really thoughtful. Every single cell in my body wished Steve was Trevor, but he wasn't. He was a great guy who, unlike Trevor, actually made an effort to make me his girlfriend. I smiled once I realized what my answer was. "Yes. I would like to be your girlfriend."

"Cool."

"Thank you for the album. You're very talented."

"Your grandpa helped me pick the shots. I thought you might want to take the memories of the Inn and your dad with you, no matter where you are. This way they will last forever."

"I love it."

"Good. Let's go." He tugged my hand to lead me out of the school.

When we got to the Inn, he leaned over the truck console to kiss me. I had caught up on all my school assignments, and there were no guests booked at the Inn, so spurred by a random impulse to take a risk, I invited Steve to my room. He'd never seen it, and I was actually feeling brave enough to make out with him. I decided to go in with an open mind and evaluate it based entirely on my feelings for Steve without my feelings for Trevor interfering—if I could. It must have taken Steve a little off guard because he seemed really nervous when we crossed the threshold. He looked around a bit and sat on my desk chair. I went into my bathroom for a minute to put in the earrings he gave me.

"Where do you watch TV?"

"I don't," I said as I leaned on the bathroom doorframe.

"Never?"

"I like reading better."

"What about movies?"

"I watch them on my laptop."

"Right." He looked around some more.

"Where are we going for dinner tomorrow? Is it romantic?"

"It's a surprise. You should wear a skirt or a dress, though." He smiled when he noticed the journal he gave me on my bedside table. "You use your journal?"

"Yeah, every night. I love it."

He lunged forward, snatching it off the table with a mischievous grinned. "What do you write about?"

"Don't." I tried to grab it from him, but he held it over his head so I couldn't reach it. I tickled his ribs and then pushed

152

him onto the bed. "Give it back or I'm going to kick you out."

He gave it back immediately without a struggle. "I don't want to get kicked out."

"Thank you." I slid the book in my desk drawer, then turned and knelt onto my bed beside him. "I don't know how far this is going to go, but—"

"I'm happy with whatever you're ready for."

I leaned in to kiss along his neck and made my way up towards his mouth. He pulled my body until I was lying on top of him. One of his hands moved along my thigh and up over my hip to my waist. His other hand cradled my neck. I closed my eyes, and as Steve's hands ran across my body, my imagination wandered. I pretended I was making out with Trevor. I couldn't help it—or maybe I could help it, and I just didn't want to. I kissed him back and touched him as if he were Trevor, and because it was something I'd been burning to do for a while, it was hot.

Steve rolled me over onto my back and leaned up on his elbow. A reminder that he was Steve not Trevor. He smiled and ran his finger along the side of my face and down my throat towards my collarbone. I could tell he wanted to draw his hand farther down to my chest, but he didn't. Instead, he placed it on my waist and leaned in to kiss me again. Interestingly, his self-control had an unexpected effect on me. The more he avoided touching me, the more I wanted him to. I didn't even have to pretend he was Trevor anymore.

I sat up, pulled my sweater over my head, and revealed the tight tank top I had on underneath. "You're so beautiful," he whispered in my ear as his phone rang in his pocket. He ignored it and kissed my neck.

A few minutes later, his phone rang again. He rolled onto his side, reached into his jeans, pulled it out of his pocket, and threw it on the floor. His fingers trailed over my hip and down the back of my leg, then he pulled my knee to drape it across his hips. His phone rang again.

"Seriously?" he asked and looked up at the ceiling as if God made his phone ring.

"Maybe you should get it," I suggested. "It might be something serious."

He inhaled deeply and sat up. He leaned over to pick it up off the floor. "Don't move," he ordered with a smile as he dialled to check his voicemail.

His face dropped and his eyebrows angled together as he listened. He stood before the message was finished. I sat up and watched him grab his jacket. He put it on with one arm as he maneuvered the phone to keep listening. After he hung up, he leaned in to kiss me. "They had to take Giselle back to the hospital in an ambulance. She's having trouble breathing. They want me to meet them there."

"Do you want me to come with you?"

"No, it's fine. It's probably just another clot. I'll call you when I know what's going on." He grinned in a very sexy way and pointed at me. "Thanks for this."

"My pleasure."

"I'll see you tomorrow for dinner."

"Okay, hold on." I stood and grabbed my sweater. "I'll walk you to the front door."

He phoned me an hour later, and it sounded like he was struggling. "Derian, can you come to the hospital? I need you."

"I'll be right there."

CHAPTER TWENTY-THREE

My granddad didn't have anyone who could cover for him at the Inn on such short notice, and with only my learner's permit, I couldn't drive without an adult in the car yet. I had to ask Trevor's dad to drive me into town to meet Steve at the hospital. I made arrangements to sleep over at Sophie's, so Jim wouldn't have to hang around waiting for me, or drive back and forth a second time.

I asked at the hospital reception desk which room Giselle was in. They sent me to the third-floor waiting room. I had never met Steve's parents, but I could tell right away the man by the door was his dad. He looked like an older version of Steve. I assumed the distraught woman in his dad's arms was his mom. Steve was hunched over on a chair in the corner with his elbows on his knees and his face buried in his hands.

I crossed the room quietly and sat on the chair beside him. When I wrapped my arms around him, he leaned towards me without even looking up. I didn't ask him what had happened because it was obviously bad. I just held him and rested my cheek on his back. We sat like that for a really long time, until a doctor came in and escorted his parents out of the room.

Steve looked over at me, his eyes red and puffy. "She died," he said.

His words slammed into my abdomen with a force that nearly made me buckle over. "What? No. She was doing better. I don't understand."

He sat back and stared at the wall, stunned. "A blot clot moved from her lungs to her brain. She had a stroke." His eyelids drooped heavily and a perplexed look crossed his face as he shook his head. "Just yesterday she was laughing. She told me what to buy you for Valentine's Day, and she made me promise I would let her style my hair for our date tomorrow."

"I'm so sorry," I said, barely audible because I was reliving the moment I found out my dad had died.

"She's gone. It's so surreal. Is this what it felt like when your dad died?"

I nodded.

"I can't believe it," he murmured. "I can't believe she's dead." He stood abruptly, grabbed the back of a chair, and flung it against the wall, breaking the glass of the picture frame. I flinched and covered my face. He threw another chair, took long strides across the room, and swung the door open so violently it dented the wall.

I ran to follow him down the hall. He made it to an emergency exit and kicked it open, which set off an alarm. He rushed down the steel exit staircase and across the parking lot. It was pouring rain. I caught up and grabbed his elbow to stop him, then wrapped my arms around his neck and held him tightly. At first, he just stood tensely, breathing heavily. Eventually, his shoulders dropped, he rested his hands on my waist, and he cried.

The funeral was three days later. Steve didn't let go of my hand until the last person left. Pretty much every person in Squamish had either attended the service or dropped by the Rawlings' house with dishes of food. It was after midnight by the time everyone left. His parents went to their room. Steve and I went to his room. I sat on the end of his bed and watched him take off his dress clothes. He didn't say anything before he went into the bathroom to get ready for bed.

"Do you want to talk?" I asked when he stepped back into the room.

He shook his head and kissed my cheek before crawling onto the mattress.

"Can I get you anything?"

He stretched his arm out so I would lie next to him. He hugged me tightly into his chest and whispered, "Thanks for being here."

I knew I was going to fall asleep, which was fine because his parents were too out of it to care if I stayed. I was supposed to be sleeping over at Sophie's anyway, so my granddad wouldn't miss me.

As I snuggled with Steve, he fell asleep. It made me remember how Trevor had slept on the floor in my room for the week after my dad died. I moved down to the condo right after the funeral and didn't talk to him for a long time. I couldn't remember ever thanking him for being there when I needed it the most.

In the morning, I snuck downstairs to make Steve breakfast. I knew he wouldn't feel like eating, but it gave me something to do. I carried a tray with a glass of orange juice and a bowl of yogurt back upstairs. His laptop was on, so I put the tray down on his desk and read all the comments about Giselle on the memorial page. I checked my email too and saw that Trevor had gotten back to me.

Hey Deri, I know you've been waiting for an update. Unfortunately, the little girl we were searching for didn't survive. The weather was bad, and we took too long to get to her. She was right where you saw her in your vision, though. You did a great job. We failed. I know you're dealing with a lot right now. You probably need a hug, and I'm sorry I'm not there for you.

Take care, Trev

There were a million things I could have written so Trevor

would know how I was doing, but in the end, it all boiled down to three words. *I miss you.* He would understand. I sent the email and crawled back into bed with Steve. He was still asleep. I kissed him on the forehead and snuggled against his chest. I cried quietly for Giselle, and the little girl in Iceland, and because life was getting really hard.

CHAPTER TWENTY-FOUR

Steve missed another three weeks of school. When he finally came back, he was still messed up. He quit student council, stopped practicing with the tennis team, ditched the casino fundraiser night, and rarely talked to anyone—including me. I felt horrible because I didn't know how to make it better for him. I decided to keep trying, even though he pushed me away each time.

Trevor only emailed once in all that time. He wrote: *Steve is lucky to have you. Take care, Trev.* It was short, but it meant a lot. It was as if he had read my mind and knew I felt like I was doing a crappy job of supporting Steve. Trevor made it look so easy when he found the right things to say to me. It wasn't easy. I tried at least fifty different angles with Steve. At best, he ignored them, and at worst, I ended up making him withdraw even more. To motivate myself to keep trying with Steve, I read Trevor's message over and over and saved it as new so it would pop up in my inbox every day. It worked.

Just before spring break, I hunted Steve down at his locker. He had gotten visibly thinner, and his hair was kind of messy, like he didn't care. "Hey," I said and kissed his cheek.

"Hey." He sighed.

"Do you want to hang out after school?"

He dropped books into his bag without much focus. "No, thanks."

"How about on the weekend?"

After he zipped his bag shut and threw it over his shoulder, he glanced at me. "I think I'm going to be pretty busy."

"Yeah? With what?"

"Stuff."

"Steve." I grabbed his elbow and glared at him. "You can start living again. It's okay to go on living. I promise. I know it doesn't feel fair that you can still do all the things your sister will never get to do again. But you have a responsibility to do them because the one thing Giselle would have asked for was to live. You've been given that gift, and you're wasting it. She's probably mad at you for not taking advantage of the one thing she misses the most."

He stared at me for a long time, and based on his expression, my speech had sunk in. Eventually, he smiled and leaned in to kiss me. "How about hiking on Saturday?"

"Perfect. I would love to go hiking on Saturday."

He stretched his arm around my waist as we turned and walked down the hall. "Thanks Deri."

I couldn't stop smiling because I finally said the right thing. It felt good to get it right. "You're welcome."

Things started going really well after that. Steve and I did things together like hiking, mountain biking, canoeing, and off-roading. We always chose something active because it kept his mind off his sister better if we didn't have to talk. I was great at coming up with adventurous outdoorsy date ideas like zip-trek-king and caving. I even convinced him we should bungee jump from the railroad bridge, but I chickened out on that one. I wasn't crazy brave. Steve started to smile and laugh again. The Inn was busier with more guest bookings. My mom and I talked on the phone at least once a week, and we actually had lots to talk about. Then, the best thing of all happened. Doug was asked to play drums with a band opening for Molten. The regular drummer broke his arm when he wiped out on his motorcycle, so Doug was scheduled to play with them for the last three dates of their tour in Vancouver, Seattle, and Los Angeles. It was a huge opportunity for him, and I was so proud. We all made plans to go downtown to watch the concert.

On the Saturday of Doug's Vancouver show, Steve came by the Inn early. We hung out in the library and played chess while we waited for Sophie and the rest of the guys from the band to pick us up in the van. He played his knight badly on purpose, so I called him on it. "Hey! Are you trying to lose?"

He smiled and sat back in the chair. "No."

"Yes you are. You don't need to do that. I can beat you fair and square."

He shook his head to disagree.

"What? You think because I'm a girl, you need to take it easy on me?"

"No. It has nothing to do with your gender."

"Then bring it on."

"Okay, you asked for it." He made three moves and I was in checkmate. I pouted and crossed my arms. "That." He pointed at my face. "Is why I don't want to beat you at chess. I don't like seeing that face."

"I can handle it. It's not like I'm a poor loser."

He laughed, not convinced, and set up the pieces again. Trevor's dad walked into the library. His expression looked too serious. My skin turned cold, as if someone had opened all the windows, ripped my clothes off, and drenched me in a bucket of icy water. My heart pounded in a demented rhythm. I knew without him even saying a word that Trevor had been hurt.

"What happened?"

Jim pressed his lips together and glanced at Steve before running his hand through his hair. Steve looked back and forth between Jim and me. He could probably feel the dread ooze out of me.

161

"Just tell me, Jim. Is he okay?"

"He had a fall."

I dug my fingers into the armrest of the chair, trying to hold on so I wouldn't collapse to the ground. "Oh my God. How bad is it?"

"I'm not sure yet. His gear failed. He fell about thirty feet into a crevasse. They needed to repel in to lift him out. Murphy's going to call again when he knows more about his injuries."

My heart alternately raced and then stopped. Each time it stopped, it made me gasp. "Why didn't I see it?" I mumbled under my breath.

Jim walked across the room and wrapped his arms around me to give me a quick hug. "I'll let you know when Murphy calls with more information." Uncomfortable with emotions, he turned and walked back out of the library.

Steve looked like he had no idea what to do. "I'm sure he'll be fine," he finally said.

Sophie and the guys pulled up in front of the Inn and honked. I stood and took a few deep breaths to collect myself. "Please, don't tell Sophie. I don't want to be a downer during Doug's big night."

We walked to the lobby, and I fought with my expression so it wouldn't show my anxiety. It must not have worked. Steve stopped me and said, "You can stay here. I'll tell her you're sick or something."

"No. I want to be there for Doug. And if I stay here by myself I'll go insane with worry."

Steve nodded and took my hand to lead me outside. I plastered on a smile when Sophie slid the van door open, but she could tell right away I was faking. "What's wrong?"

"Nothing." I hopped in and sat in the back row.

Sophie made eye contact with Steve to see if he would spill it. He just smiled and sat next to me. Sophie glanced back and forth between us but eventually turned and slid the van door shut again.

When we got to the arena, she pulled me into the bathroom and stared me down. "What's going on?"

"Nothing. This is Doug's big night. Let's just have fun."

"Deri."

Not able to lie any longer, I caved. "Trevor fell while he was climbing. I don't know how bad his injuries are."

"Shit." She leaned her butt against the sink.

"I don't understand why I didn't see it before it happened. I could have warned him."

"Maybe it's a good sign you didn't have a Spidey-sense beforehand. It means it wasn't serious."

"I don't know. My intuition isn't exactly reliable."

"You definitely would have felt something if he was in real danger."

I nodded and let hope sink in. I wanted her theory to be true. If she was right, it meant he was fine. "Okay." I took a deep breath to calm down. "There's nothing I can do about it right now anyway. Jim said he would update me once he knew more. Let's just enjoy the concert."

After thinking about it, she sighed, then nodded and we went to our seats. The show rocked and we were invited back stage. I had never seen Doug so pumped. I tried really hard to hold it together, but he knew as soon as he hugged me. "What's wrong, Deri?"

"Nothing. You were awesome. I'm so proud of you."

"Why are you trembling?"

"I guess because it was such a rush to see you up on stage at a real concert."

He held my shoulders. "Why are you upset?"

"It's nothing, Doug, really. Enjoy your moment." My phone rang. "Excuse me." I ran to a door and stepped out into a corridor, where it was quiet. "Hello." All I could hear was crackling and realized it was because I was in the concrete arena. The signal wasn't coming through. I ran to the nearest exit and burst out the door.

"Deri?" Murphy asked.

"Yeah. How is he?" My eyes clenched shut as I braced for the answer.

"Broken ribs, a collapsed lung, some deep lacerations that needed stitches, and a concussion."

"So, he's going to be okay?"

"Eventually." He chuckled. "Both his body and ego are going to be sore for a while."

Relieved, I exhaled and crouched down on the sidewalk. "Can I talk to him?" There was a long silence on the other end of the phone. I thought maybe we got disconnected. "Murph?"

"He doesn't know I called. He asked me not to call you."

"Why?"

There was another long silence. "He doesn't want to talk to you." My breath stuttered as if I'd been kicked in the chest. Obviously Murphy could hear my sobs because he said, "Deri. He's just—"

"Save it. I don't want to hear it. Thanks for letting me know." I hung up and tried to get back inside the arena. The door was locked, so I had to text Steve to come save me.

He opened the door from the inside and asked, "How is he?"

"Fine." I stepped in and placed my hands on his chest to push him back towards the wall. He smiled as I ran my palms over his shoulders and down his arms. "Kiss me."

He clutched my hair and our lips collided. I was really upset that Trevor didn't want to talk to me and that's why I let Steve touch me the way he did. If Sophie hadn't interrupted to tell us that everyone was heading out, I might have let him do whatever he wanted.

CHAPTER TWENTY-FIVE

A week after the concert, Steve and I went to his room to make out. A few minutes into it, I noticed he wasn't kissing me back with the same intensity. It seemed as if he was hesitating. Then he threw a total curve ball I hadn't seen coming—maybe I was in denial and hadn't wanted to see it coming. He said, "I love you, Derian."

The first thing that attempted to come out of my mouth was, *What?* Fortunately, I pressed my lips together and it didn't escape. I racked my brain to generate possible responses and quickly calculate the repercussions of each of the alternatives. Obviously, *I love you too,* was the logical and simplest response, but I didn't feel that way. I loved him in the sense that I cared about him. I just didn't love him in the sense that he wanted me to.

Thanks, cool, I'm glad, I'm happy to hear that, I'm the luckiest girl in the world. All my ideas sounded lame, so I panicked. The seconds ticked by and my mouth went dry from the fear. Say nothing—that was my only viable option.

I leaned towards him to give him a good angle to see my cleavage in my cute pink push-up bra. I lingered for a while, then leaned in and closed the gap between our mouths. He wrapped his arms tightly around my body and rolled me onto my back. I was very pleased with myself for successfully dodging the response. He ran his hand over my cute pink push-up bra and looked me directly in the eye. "I love you," he repeated.

Shit. Obviously, I wasn't that good at distracting him. "I know," I finally said and cringed as soon as the words came out of my mouth.

He sat up. I didn't even try to apologize because I knew it would make everything worse.

He threw my shirt onto my lap and walked to his bedroom door. "Come on, I'll take you home."

"Don't you want to talk about this?"

He laughed, but not in a happy way. "No, Derian, I don't want to talk about how I love you and you don't love me."

"I care about you."

His lip snarled a little. "That's nice, Deri. Thanks."

"Maybe it just takes me longer to fall in love."

"We both know that's not the problem."

Knowing exactly what he meant, I got up and pulled my shirt on. I grabbed my bag and we drove back to the Inn in silence. When he parked out front, he turned the engine off and sighed. He didn't say anything, but I could tell he wanted to, so I waited. Two men in suits exited the Inn and examined the exterior of the building for a while before they got into a Lexus SUV.

Steve turned his head to face me. His expression flickered with different emotions, as if there was some sort of battle going on inside him. I waited for him to speak and when he didn't I said, "Thanks for being patient with me."

"Sure." His tone was abrupt and completely unconvincing.

There was no point trying to repair the damage while he was still hurt. If it was even possible to repair it. I said goodbye, got out of the truck, and walked through the front door of the Inn. I couldn't tell how I felt. Steve was the first guy who had ever told me he loved me. I should have been excited, but I just felt confused.

My granddad was at the front desk. When he saw me he smiled in a sympathetic way. "Why the long face?" he asked.

I inhaled deeply and leaned my elbows on the front desk. I thought for a long time, then mumbled, "I miss Trevor."

"Ah. So does Kailyn. She's in the dining room making him a card. Maybe you should make one too."

"Who were those men?"

He glanced at my face, then sorted some receipts. "Developers."

I frowned and my eyes got watery. "Do they want to keep the building or demolish it?"

"They're thinking demolition."

"What did you tell them?"

"I said I would think about it."

"Okay." I couldn't breathe very well. I gave him a hug, then turned towards the dining room. "I'll make dinner tonight," I said over my shoulder.

Kailyn was set up with her craft box at a table near the window, so I pulled up a chair. "Hi Deri. Do you think Trevor will like this?" She held up a folded piece of purple construction paper covered in happy faces and gold sprinkles.

"He's going to love it."

"Do you think Trevor is going to stay away forever like my mom?"

"No. He's coming back. He would never leave you."

She nodded and added hearts to her card. "My mom doesn't love me because of my Down syndrome. I was a bad baby, so she left."

Trevor never talked about why his mom left, but what I did know was he never got over being mad at her. She made efforts to have contact with them over the years, which seemed to go okay when we were all young, but something happened when Trevor was about thirteen. He wanted nothing to do with his mom after that and wouldn't let Kailyn anywhere near her. I always wished I knew the whole story. "That's not why she left. You were a good baby."

"Why did she leave?"

"I don't know, Kiki, but it wasn't because she didn't love you and Trevor."

She added more glitter. "Trevor loves me more because I'm special. I love Trevor and you."

"We love you too. He will always come back for you. Don't ever worry that he won't."

"Okay. Do you miss Trevor?"

I nodded and emotion rose up into my throat. "Do you mind if I make a card too?"

She handed me a stick of glue and a pack of pencil crayons. "I'll help you with your spelling."

I smiled. "Thanks."

I rummaged through her tote of art supplies and found a thick piece of white card stock. I sketched a picture of Britannia with the Mavertys' house, the Inn, and the mountain in the background. I added really small details including our tree fort in the forest; his 4Runner parked out front; his work boots sitting by the bench on his front porch; and the T.M. + D.L. carved into the railing of the Inn. I used her pencil crayons to make it look like the light was on in his bedroom window and then I wrote on the back: *It's not the same around here without you.*

"That's good, Derian."

"Thanks. Do you want to stay for dinner? I'm going to make chicken and baby potatoes."

"Okay. Can Daddy come too?"

"Of course. We can have a nice family dinner together." Right after I spoke, I had a vision.

Two people were doing it in a bedroom that didn't look familiar. The guy was Steve.

I abruptly opened my eyes. I had never even seen something that graphic in a movie, so it was quite shocking that my mind created the images.

"What did you see in your mind?"

Once I recovered, I said, "People kissing."

She giggled as she addressed the envelope. "Were they going to make a baby?"

"It appeared that way." Since I couldn't erase the image from my brain, I changed the subject to distract myself. "How are things going with you and Evan?"

"He kissed Daisy Edwards on the lips. I don't want to marry him anymore."

"I'm sorry. I'm sure you'll meet someone new."

"I already did. Jonathan Kensington. He works at the Tim Horton's and wants me to be his girlfriend."

I smiled and added a few more details to my drawing. "Trevor's going to want to meet him."

"No. He doesn't have to. I said no to Jonathan." She meticulously colour-coded all her felt pens into their case. "I'm too busy for a boyfriend. I'm going to be a librarian assistant. I have college classes to go to."

"Really? That's great. I didn't know you were doing that."

She took a sip from her glass of milk. "That's because you never hang out with me anymore."

I winced from the guilt. "Sorry. I'll make it up to you. We can do more things together."

"Will you call my mom and ask her to come visit me?"

"I don't know her number."

"Trevor does. You said you would get it from him. That was a long time ago. You promised."

It had completely slipped my mind that I had promised I would try to get it, so I made up an excuse, which was also the truth. "I didn't promise. I said I would try. Trevor doesn't think it's a good idea to call your mom."

"Why?"

"I don't know. He's never told me why."

I watched her stick more stars to her card. She sniffled and when she looked up, there were tears in her eyes. There was nothing more heartbreaking than seeing Kailyn cry. It rarely happened because Trevor always worked really hard to make sure nothing made her sad. She wiped the back of her hand over her eyelids and said, "She's my mom. I want to see her."

It was painful for me too because I completely related to that loneliness. I gave her a hug and said, "I'll see what I can do." I finished making my card, then went into the kitchen to start dinner. While it was cooking, I headed to my room and searched through my albums for a photograph to add to the package for Trevor. I found one of him, Kailyn and me in a rowboat when we were really little. My dad had taken the picture. We all had huge grins, with our little red life jackets on. Trevor was pulling the oars and I was waving at my dad. It was cute.

Jim and my granddad were already seated at the table in the dining room with Kailyn when I returned. I slipped the photo into the envelope and headed into the kitchen to prepare the plates for dinner.

As I served them, Jim asked, "So, has Trevor been writing you a thousand times a day?"

"No. He's only written three times."

Jim looked genuinely surprised. "Oh. I assumed—" He cleared his throat. "Kailyn, would you pass the beans, please."

Kailyn passed the dish and said, "Trevor writes me every day to tell me all about Iceland. There is a volcano and hardly any animals, just foxes and rabbits and goats and sheep. Murphy saw a polar bear, though. It floated on the ice and stopped for a visit. They speak Icelandic there, but Trevor and Murphy don't understand, so everyone says things in English for them. He's almost better from his fall. He says he can't remember if it hurt when he landed because he bumped his head and he forgot."

"Has he been writing you every day too?" I asked Jim.

He shrugged, reluctant to admit it to me since I'd only gotten three messages. "Yeah, but he mostly just tells me about the rescues they've gone on."

Knowing it was about work stuff made me feel a little less

170

like the odd man out. "It's so sad about the little girl, eh?"

"Which little girl?"

"The one they didn't get to in time." I chose my words carefully because I didn't want to upset Kailyn. I was surprised Jim didn't know what I was talking about. It was kind of a big deal.

"They lost one?"

"Didn't he tell you?"

"No. What happened?"

I told the story and watched Jim's expression.

"Did the little girl go to heaven?" Kailyn asked me.

I glanced at her. I wanted to lie, but I couldn't. "Yes."

"Don't worry, your dad and granny will take good care of her."

Touched by that image, I looked back at Jim. "Why do you think he didn't tell you?"

"Well." He shifted uncomfortably in his chair and raised one eyebrow. His eyes got shiny the same way Trevor's did when he was choked up. "Those are tough calls to talk about. I've still never told anyone about the first kid I lost." He stood up with a stack of dirty dishes and kissed the top of my head. "He's lucky to have you. Thanks for dinner."

I watched Jim disappear into the kitchen and thought about what he said. I couldn't understand why Trevor would confide in me when it was really important but avoid me in every other way. I took the rest of the dishes to the kitchen and vigorously scrubbed them in the sink, trying to figure out what was going on in Trevor's head. I always thought I knew him so well, but he was acting out of character. I didn't know what any of it meant.

I went to my room and turned on my laptop to write him a message.

Hey Trev, either we're friends or we're not. Why are you sending emails to everyone but me? Why didn't you want to talk to me after your fall? Why did you try to leave without even saying goodbye? Why did you ask Doug to keep an eye on me, but then you don't even check in to see how I'm doing? Sometimes you act as if I mean something special to you. The rest of the time you act as if you want nothing to do with me. I don't get it. I thought I knew how your mind worked, but now I'm completely confused. Do you love me more than a sister? If you don't, why not? If you do, what are you waiting for? Steve told me he loves me. Do you care? I love you. Screw you. Stay safe.

I stared at the message on my computer screen for a long time. My finger hovered over the mouse, waiting for my brain to get the nerve to press the send button. My finger finally moved, but it was to erase everything I wrote. He didn't need the annoyance of an immature high-school drama queen whining about why he didn't love her back. When did I become so insecure? Disgusted with myself, I turned the computer off and went to bed.

CHAPTER TWENTY-SIX

Sophie and Doug and I went skiing the next day, and I was acting weird. I knew it. My pornographic vision starring Steve was freaking me out. I was not ready for anything close to what I saw him doing.

"What the hell's wrong with you?" Sophie asked when we went into the chalet to use the washroom.

After she came out of the cubicle, I whispered, "I had a vision that made it seem like my relationship with Steve is going to take a dramatic leap forward. I'm afraid to even be alone with him."

"What'd you see?"

"It was vulgar. I'll spare you the details."

"No, I like details."

The other girl who was in the washroom left, so I hopped up and sat on the counter as Sophie put more eyeliner on. "Watch a porno, you'll get the idea. It's probably more important for me to mention that he told me he loves me in real life."

"Holy shit! Did you say it back?"

"No. I didn't say anything, so he said it again. I didn't know what to do and responded by saying, 'I know.'"

"You didn't."

"I did."

She laughed. "Classic. You're such a dork."

"What was I supposed to do? I wasn't going to lie."

She removed her toque and combed her fingers through her hair. "People say it all the time without meaning it."

"Did you mean it when you first told Doug?"

"Yeah, but in the eighth grade I told Gavin I loved him because I felt sorry for him."

I shook my head and hopped off the counter. "That doesn't count. Thirteen-year-olds don't know what love is."

"Do seventeen-year-olds?"

"Does anyone?" I joked.

She waved her hand to indicate I was over thinking it. "You saw it happening in the future. That doesn't mean it's going to happen today. It could be months or years from now. Maybe it wasn't even you."

"True, since it's safe to assume he hates me right now. The girl had long brown hair like mine, though."

"Stay away from alcohol. You should be all right."

As we headed back outside to meet Doug, I asked, "How's it going with your parents now that your dad moved back in?"

"Good. The counsellor has them going on dates when my dad's not flying. If he's away on an overnight he has to send her a love email. They're ridiculously cheesy."

"You read them?"

"Yeah. My mom doesn't know how to check her email and she refuses to learn. I have to do everything for her."

"You might end up traumatizing yourself if you read about something kinky."

"Good point. I'll stop."

Doug was seated on the railing of the chalet porch, waiting for us. As we walked towards him, I said, "I need to borrow him again, if you don't mind. We won't be getting it on. I just need him to do something illegal for me."

"He's all yours. Thanks for telling me." She draped her arm

over my shoulder. "You can make out with him a little if you want."

"Ha ha. His hacking services should be sufficient."

Mason and a group of guys and girls from our school took their skis off and headed onto the chalet porch. Mason sported titanium sunglasses, a twelve-hundred-dollar, royal-blue, heated ski jacket, and Apex boots that cost just as much. He could have seriously been a model. Maybe he was, for all I knew. Or royalty, or something.

"Still crushing on Mr. One-Night Stand?" Doug asked, since I had been in a complete daze watching Mason.

Although I was, I said, "I think it's time for me to swear off boys."

That Monday at school, Mason hobbled past me on crutches. His knee was in a brace. It was a struggle for him to carry his books and maneuver the crutches at the same time. Nobody offered to help him, so I spent a few minutes coming up with conversation-starters, then stood next to his locker. He hopped on one foot to keep his balance. The crutches slid across the door and clattered to the floor, which gave me the excuse I was looking for. So much for swearing off boys. I stepped forward and picked them up for him. "Hey. Would you like some help?"

He smiled appreciatively. "Sure, thanks."

"Here, I'll take your books. You can take these." I passed the crutches to him as he handed me his books. "I'm Derian."

He smiled again and said, "Yeah, I remember from when Nikolai introduced us. Mason." He held his hand out to shake mine. I adjusted his books to put my hand into his, feeling stupid for sounding like I hadn't remembered already being introduced. He had the smoothest skin I had ever felt on a male, or a female for that matter.

"Did you hurt your knee skiing?"

"No." His eyebrow lifted as he likely contemplated how I had

175

known he'd been skiing. "I took an awkward hit in hockey last night."

"Where are you headed?" I asked, just so I wouldn't look like a wack job who already knew his schedule.

"A-wing."

"Me too." I walked slowly. He alternately stepped and pushed off the crutches. "How long do you have to be on crutches?"

"The doctor said a couple of weeks—longer if I need surgery."

"I can be your personal assistant until you're back on your feet, if you want."

What kind of ridiculous thing was that to say? Being able to speak in front of him was definitely a sign of my growth, but the conversation content was sadly deficient. He dropped his chin and grinned in a shy way. It was insanely cute. He didn't actually take me up on my offer. He might have thought I was joking, or maybe he didn't want me tagging along with him everywhere. He stopped and held out his arm to take his books back. I looked up and realized we had already arrived at his classroom door. I was disappointed that the entire interaction had flown by that quickly. "Thanks Derian. It's a beautiful name, by the way. I wouldn't have called you Kefir if I knew you in elementary school."

I laughed, surprised and pleased he remembered that. "Thanks."

Neither one of us made a motion to leave.

Arms wrapped around my waist from behind and Steve said, "Hey, babe." Apparently he was over the *I love you* diss.

I glanced over my shoulder at him and then back at Mason. Mason had already turned on his crutches and was trying to rock himself forward. "See you around, Derian," he said. The door hit him in the shoulder as he disappeared into his class.

"I didn't know you and Cartwright were friends."

I stepped away from Steve's embrace. "We're not. I carried his books because he's on crutches. I was being nice, is that a problem?"

176

Steve frowned, taken back by my attitude. "No. I love that you're nice to everyone."

"Are you sure?"

He looked confused since he was the one with a reason to be mad, but I was the one who was acting snappy. "I'm just surprised you would spend time with someone like him."

"What exactly do you mean when you say 'someone like him'?"

"He's like all his rich friends—pretentious, shallow, and selfish."

"That's weird because he volunteered for the food drive, and the Guatemala fundraiser, and he tutors his grade-eight neighbour."

He studied my expression as what I said sunk in. "I thought you didn't know him."

"You thought you did. I can talk to whomever I want to."

"I know. I didn't say you couldn't. Are you mad at me for some reason?"

"I'm going to be late. I'll see you later." I turned without kissing him, crossed the hall, and ducked into my classroom.

I texted Doug: *Can you meet me after school?*

Does Sophie know?

Yes

Meet me at my car.

k. thanks.

Doug was already sitting in his car when I walked up and slid into the passenger seat. "Sophie said we can make out."

He turned his head and nodded as if he was fine with that. "Too bad Trevor would kick my ass. Otherwise, I would take her up on that hall pass."

"Yeah right. I need you to find Trevor's mom's phone number."

"Why don't you just ask him?"

"He won't give it to me because it's for his sister. He doesn't want Kailyn talking to their mom."

He turned in his seat to face me. "Why?"

"I don't know. She did some things he won't tell me about. He thinks he's protecting Kailyn from getting hurt."

177

"If he thinks it's not a good idea, then it's probably not a good idea." He reached into the inside pocket of his leather jacket for a pack of gum. He chewed gum whenever he had a craving to smoke a cigarette, which was pretty much constantly.

"She has a right to contact her mom if she wants to. Will you help?"

"No." He held out the pack of gum to offer me a piece.

"Seriously?"

"I don't want to get involved. If Trevor thinks Kailyn will get hurt by talking to her mom, I don't want to be a part of that. You shouldn't either."

"She's sad, Doug. It hurts me to see her that sad." I mimicked the puppy-dog pout that Sophie used on him. "Please."

He rolled his eyes. "That look is not going to work. The answer is no. Sorry."

"Fine. Be that way. I'll figure it out myself." I stuck my tongue out at him so he would know I wasn't really mad at him. "See you tomorrow."

I got out of his car and heard him say, "don't meddle," as I closed the car door. Steve was standing with his back against the wall, arms crossed. He didn't look happy.

I walked over to him. "Hey."

"What's going on, Deri?"

"Nothing. Doug is helping me with a project."

"What was with the attitude earlier?"

"I was feeling grumpy. Sorry."

"So, we're good?"

"Of course," I mumbled and kept walking.

CHAPTER TWENTY-SEVEN

Things weren't great between Steve and me because I knew he wanted more. It was too stressful to pretend we were cool when we weren't. It was impacting my grades, so I told him I needed a break from hanging out so I could study for exams. It was my lame, chicken-shit, and horribly immature way of breaking up with him.

I treated the mission to find Kailyn and Trevor's mom like a research project, and after a few hours of digging, and one white lie to the receptionist at her country club, I got a phone number for her. Having the information in my hand triggered second thoughts, and I didn't share it with Kailyn right away. It wasn't until I found her crying on their porch one day that I finally caved in and gave it to her. It made her so happy, she literally skipped into the house to use the phone. I hung out to eavesdrop, just to be sure it went okay. As it turned out, Lorraine didn't answer. Kailyn left a message and then hugged me to thank me.

The third Saturday in June I took the bus down and spent the day in Vancouver with my mom. I thought it was probably a good idea to work on finding some common ground with her before I had to move. For some reason, as soon as I was near her, my back got up and I became defensive, even though she hadn't even said anything confrontational. It was my suggestion that maybe I should go back to the counsellor to figure out what my problem was. She was completely supportive of that idea. No surprise.

It was after eight o'clock when I returned to the Inn. Granddad handed me a letter that had come in the regular mail for me. It was from Trevor. At first, I was excited, but then my heart felt as if it collapsed on itself when I saw what was inside. He had sent back the sketch of Britannia I drew. It seemed unnecessarily cruel. If he didn't want it, he could have just thrown it out. I didn't understand why he had to return it. I slammed it down on the desk.

Granddad picked it up, wondering what was up with my outburst. "Did you draw this?"

"Yeah, I sent it to Trevor. He sent it back. He's an idiot."

Granddad held up the picture and examined the detail. "I'm sure he sent it home so it wouldn't get lost over there."

That's when I noticed Trevor's handwriting under my message on the underside. "Oh. I take back what I said. He's not an idiot. I didn't see his message until you held it up."

He flipped the card over. "Aw, that's nice. There you go."

After he went into the library, I ran my finger over Trevor's handwriting. I re-read my message: *It's not the same around here without you.* Then, I read his response about fifty times: *I don't ever want to be missing from this picture again. I'll be home on June 30th. Can't wait. Please keep this for me. I want it when I get home.*

Even though I had no hopes that his feelings would have magically changed while he was gone, I was still really excited to see him. My phone buzzed with a message from Sophie:

Are you home from your mom's yet? Murphy's brother is having a party at his house tonight. You're coming.

No thanks. Steve will probably be there.

Good. It will give you a chance to grow a pair and actually tell him he's not your boyfriend anymore. You don't want to be that girl who leaves a guy hanging because she's a wuss, do you?

I sighed heavily, knowing she was right. *Fine.*

I showered and dressed in dark jeans and a T-shirt. High ponytail. No make-up. I clipped the chain with my dad's wedding ring on it around my neck and looked in the mirror. In some ways I had changed a lot since moving back. In some ways I was the same old Derian, and honestly, I liked her.

In the lobby, my granddad gave me the keys to his car, reluctantly. I had passed my exam to graduate from a learner's permit to a novice license, but it was the first time I was going to drive by myself at night. "I'll be careful."

"I know you will. It's everyone else on the road I'm worried about."

"I don't want to live my entire life scared like Mom."

"I don't want that either." He hugged me. "I love you."

"I love you too. Don't worry."

It was almost ten-thirty when I finally parked down the street from Murphy and Ryan's house. I could hear the band playing from a block away. Steve's Explorer was parked right behind Mason's Mercedes. I walked along the sidewalk, then stopped at the end of the driveway and took deep breaths to make the panicky feeling go away. It shouldn't have been that difficult. It wasn't as if I was sparing his feelings by stringing him along. The respectful and grown-up thing to do was be honest and let him move on.

After a steeling breath, I carried on towards the house to do the right thing.

"Deri!" Murphy's booming voice startled me. He lunged forward and swung me around in a big bear hug.

"Oh my God! What are you doing here? Welcome home." The fact that he shouldn't be home hit me. "Is Trevor home too? I thought you were coming home on the thirtieth."

"He told you that so he could surprise you." His eyebrow lifted and he smiled. "Surprise." He reached into the open window of his truck to get his phone off the dashboard. "Let's go inside. He's been dying to see you."

Holy shit. I wasn't prepared. In my imagination, our reunion consisted of me running and launching myself into his arms. In private. Even without that particular scenario, it would be awkward to greet him in front of an entire party full of people. Steve was already there. "Um, maybe I should let him have time with his friends. I can see him tomorrow in Britannia."

Murphy's expression changed and he glanced back at the house. "He wants to see you, Deri. Trust me."

"He didn't even want to talk to me after his fall." I bit my bottom lip, because the reminder stung.

Murphy grinned in a funny way. "Get inside. You'll feel better once you see him. Besides, I won't live if he finds out you were here and I let you go home without at least saying hello. He's been whining about missing you for five months. If you don't walk in there on your own I'll throw you over my shoulder and carry you in."

Trevor whining about anything seemed highly unlikely. He wasn't really the *share your feelings openly* type. I stood staring at the house and took a deep breath, twisting my hair around my finger. Sophie must have known they were here when she told me to come over. Those types of surprises were not a good idea. Not for me anyway. Officially breaking up with Steve and reuniting with Trevor in front of a whole crowd of people. Not really ideal conditions for either event. "Ask him to come out—"

"That's it—you're coming with me." Murphy scooped me up and bent me over his broad shoulder.

"No Murphy! Let me go!" I screamed, smacked his back, and wiggled my legs. It made no difference. He was way too strong.

He walked up the front steps, kicked the door open, and shouted, "Look who I found."

Everyone within a twenty-foot radius gawked at us. Once

Murphy put me down, I saw Trevor immediately. He was across the room, and smiled before weaving through the people to make his way to me. Even though he was in his standard black T-shirt and dark jeans, he looked even sexier than I remembered. I assumed he was going to give me a big hug and swing me around, but he didn't. He clutched my hand, lead me down the hall, and into a room for privacy. He closed the door and pulled me close as if we were dancing. My cheek rested on his chest and it felt incredibly comforting as his body rose with each breath. "Welcome home," I whispered.

He didn't say anything, so I tilted my head to look at him. He was choked up. His eyes were definitely shiny, and his face tensed as he tried to keep it together. Knowing that he was emotional over our reunion made me love him even more—which I hadn't thought was possible. My heart bounced around like a rubber ball inside my chest. He slid his hands until he was holding either side of my neck and stared into my eyes for a long time.

Please kiss me. Please kiss me. Please kiss me, I prayed. *Shit.* What was I doing? Steve would be crushed if he knew what I was wishing for.

"New earrings?" Trevor ran his thumb over one of the gold hearts Steve had given me.

"I've had them for a while."

"They look nice on you."

"Thanks," I murmured. He obviously knew they were a gift from Steve, so I added, "They're not quite my taste."

"I know." He leaned forward and rested his forehead on mine. His eyes were closed and his breathing was slow at first. As his palm slid down my body and found my hand, his breathing sped up. He parted his lips slightly and wrapped his fingers tightly around mine. His other hand moved up my arm, over my shoulder, and then he slid his fingers into my hair.

It felt like something was about to happen. I wanted something to happen. But not with Steve in the next room. Trevor must have sensed my hesitation because he said, "Steve's probably wondering where you are."

"Probably," I whispered.

He stepped backwards until his shoulders leaned against the door but still held my hand.

I stared at my feet for a while to work up the courage to ask, "Why didn't you email me more?"

He frowned and closed his eyes for a long blink. "I thought it would make it easier for you."

"Really? It didn't."

He chuckled at my tone. "I guess it was easier for me. Because I missed you. The sketch of Britannia made me so homesick, I grabbed my bag and I was going to hop on the next plane home."

"Why didn't you want to talk to me after you fell?"

"Because I knew how worried you would be. If you asked me to come home, I would have."

Oh. That was the perfect answer. Even though I didn't know if it meant what I wanted it to mean, it made me feel fiercely close to him. I stepped forward and rested my entire body on his. He wrapped his arms around me. I literally could have stood that way listening to his heartbeat all night.

"People are going to start rumours if we don't go back out to the party." He gently moved me so my weight wasn't rested against him. Then he opened the door and guided me by the shoulders back down the hall.

We walked into the living room and Murphy winked. Trevor draped his arm over my shoulder. I wrapped my arm around his waist and pressed the side of my body against his. He turned his head and looked down at me for a second, but a friend of his arrived at the party, so he stepped away from me and moved his arm to shake the guy's hand. I watched his mouth as he talked to the guy. He must have felt me staring because he smiled and, without looking at me, he extended his arm to hold my hand. I looked around the room, trying to spot Steve. I needed to speak to him privately and formally break up with him, quickly.

Trevor's phone beeped with a text message and he frowned a little. "Excuse me for a minute, Jessie. I have to take this." He turned towards me and pulled me into his chest with one arm. He dialled with his other hand and kissed my forehead while he waited for the call to connect. He was warm and he smelled so familiar. "Hey… Yeah, Why? Okay… No. I'll head home… Okay, I'll be right there." He hung up and inhaled in a stressful way.

"What's wrong?"

"Kailyn's been crying non-stop for two hours. She won't tell my dad what's wrong. He's hoping maybe she'll talk to me. I should probably get going."

"I'll come too. Maybe it's a girl thing." I glanced over at the band. They were set up in the dining room. "I just need to talk to Sophie real quick after they finish their set. I can meet you at your house."

"Yeah, okay." He grabbed his keys off a bookshelf, hugged me one more time, and left out the front door.

The crash of a microphone slamming against the floor made me jump. It was followed by the high-pitched screech of feedback. I spun around in time to see Sophie jump into the crowd in the sunken living room.

"Shit." I pushed past people to get to her.

CHAPTER TWENTY-EIGHT

Sophie was all up in Lisa Alvarez's face, telling her to leave the party or get her ass kicked. Steve stepped in between them and Sophie slapped him. Lisa shot me a self-satisfied smirk and then strutted past me to leave the party.

Sophie snapped at Steve, "Tell her or I will."

Steve looked like he was going to be sick. I walked over to him. "What the hell is going on?" I asked in a hushed voice.

Doug glared at us and growled, "Tell her."

I grabbed Steve's hand, pulled him out onto the deck, and shut the sliding glass door behind us. "What was all that about?"

He winced and hid his face with his hands.

"Are you hurt?"

"No."

"What's going on, Steve?"

"I fucked up."

"What do mean?"

"You're going to hate me."

"Why?"

He swallowed hard and took a while to respond, "I was hanging out with Rhys last night. We were at his house playing pool and

I had a few beers." He stopped talking and looked at me with the strangest expression.

"What happened?"

"Some more people came over. It turned into a party. I'm so sorry, Deri."

"Why?"

"I got really drunk."

"And?"

He leaned his head back and looked up at the sky.

"What did you do, Steve?"

He blinked and squeezed his eyelids tightly. "I slept with Lisa Alvarez. I'm so sorry, Derian. I don't even really remember what happened."

The vision of him doing it with a girl with long brown hair flashed through my mind. Vividly. It was unfortunate that I knew exactly what he'd done. "Well, you've made this part easy." I took the earrings out and placed them into his palm. "We're officially done. Sorry I wasn't a better girlfriend." I turned on my heel, not waiting for his reaction. Everyone stared at me as I stepped back into the house. "I'll call you when I get home," I said to Sophie. Then I walked right out the front door and down the sidewalk towards my granddad's car.

Mason was next to his car, unlocking the door. "You okay?"

I shrugged, not exactly sure. Although I did feel on the brink of tears, I technically shouldn't have been upset. Only a few minutes before it happened, I was in the bedroom with Trevor. I wanted things to be over with Steve. Then I found out he cheated on me, and I was hurt. It was hypocritical to be offended. And stupid.

Mason studied my expression and appeared genuinely concerned. "Do you need a ride back to Britannia?"

Surprised he knew I didn't live in Squamish, I shook my head and tucked my hair behind my ears. "I'm fine, thanks. I have my granddad's car here."

He gestured with his arm to indicate he would walk me to my car. "Steve's an idiot," he said as we headed down the sidewalk.

I shrugged again, uncomfortable that people were going to blame Steve when it was just as much my fault. "Our relationship was pretty much over anyway."

"I can't believe he threw away what he had with you for Lisa Alvarez. He's going to regret that for the rest of his life."

I stopped once we reached my granddad's car and leaned my butt on the driver's door. "You enjoyed the company of Lisa Alvarez, too, if my memory serves me correctly."

He chuckled. "I would never cheat on a girlfriend—especially not a girlfriend like you. He's an idiot."

I frowned, wondering what he meant by *a girlfriend like you*. It was sweet but hard to accept as a compliment since he didn't know me or what kind of girlfriend I was. "You don't have to say nice things just because I got humiliated in front of everyone."

"Nobody will think any less of you. Steve's the one who made the biggest mistake of his life."

Embarrassed he overstated the truth, I stared down at my shoes. "Well, thank you for the inflated compliments, but I think the best way to salvage my self-esteem is to go home and pretend it never happened."

"The compliments weren't inflated."

Our eyes met, and his expression was completely sincere, which made my face heat up. "Thank you," I said, turning to hide my blush and unlock the door. "I should get home."

He held the door open for me. "Drive safe."

I nodded and then snuck one more glance at his shy smile. There was definitely no mystery to why he had so many admirers, but I didn't need any more practice boyfriends. Trevor was home, and I was ready to go for it. "Thanks, Mason. Bye."

I drove home completely focused on the road, partly because everything that had happened was too overwhelming to think about, and partly because I didn't want to crash on my first solo trip.

Trevor was on his porch waiting for me when I drove up and parked. "Murphy called to tell me what happened. Are you okay?" he asked.

"Yeah. I guess. I will be. How's Kailyn?"

"She's still pretty upset, and I don't know why, so I should go back inside."

"Do you think it would help if I talked to her?"

"Maybe tomorrow." He ran his hand through his hair, not at all as relaxed as he had been at the party. "Text me if you need anything."

"Okay." I hesitated and pumped myself up to make a grand gesture. "You can come over after she falls asleep. If you want."

His eyes met mine, then his gaze darted away. "It will probably be pretty late. I'll see you in the morning."

Still feeling brave, or maybe it was desperate, I threw out another offer. "Do you want to go hiking in the morning?"

He nodded slowly as if the decision required a ton of contemplation. "Sure. Everyone is going to the springs. Bring your bathing suit. But I want one of your homemade breakfasts first."

"You got it."

He winked and went into his house.

CHAPTER TWENTY-NINE

I woke up at four-forty-five in the morning, before my alarm even rang, excited to go hiking with Trevor. I pulled my hair into a high ponytail and dressed in short shorts and a tank top over my bikini.

The dining room started to smell delicious as the water gurgled through the coffee-maker and the muffins baked in the kitchen. Granddad joined me at seven-thirty to help clear tables and serve coffee and juice. When the door chimes rang at eight, I knew it was Trevor, and I felt a tingly sensation buzz through my body. I turned to watch him enter the dining room. He had on black shorts and a grey T-shirt with his red baseball hat on backwards. He smiled and said, "Morning, sunshine."

"Morning." Wow. Just being around him did things to me that I never felt from Steve. Or anyone. "Help yourself." I pointed to the buffet table.

"Mmm. I can't believe I survived five months without your breakfasts."

"They're nothing fancy."

"Doesn't have to be fancy to be good," he said as he piled fruit, two boiled eggs, and French toast on his plate.

After Trevor finished eating, he helped me wash dishes in the kitchen. Then we left out of the kitchen door. A man in khakis and a sweater was crouched on the side porch, examining the wood. He shook the handrail to test its sturdiness. "May I help you?" I asked.

"Oh, good morning. You must be Derian." He offered his hand to shake mine. "My name is Alan. I've been trying to talk your grandfather into selling me the Inn." He reached over and shook Trevor's hand. Trevor introduced himself, and the man pointed at the heart Trevor and I had carved in the porch post when we were very young. "The T. M. of T. M. + D. L. in this heart?"

"That would be me," Trevor said, sounding proud of that fact. We both smiled and exchanged a glance at the memory of carving the heart with Jim's fishing knife when we were six and eight. Granddad was so mad, but Grandma wouldn't let him replace the post because she thought it was adorable. Our punishment was to hand wash all the breakfast dishes at the Inn for an entire week of summer holidays. Needless to say, I never vandalized again.

"So, Derian, your grandfather says you're concerned a developer will demolish the Inn and build a big resort, but my wife and I have actually been looking for quite some time to buy a heritage Inn we could raise our kids in. We will operate it essentially the same as you do now. We don't want to see it demolished any more than you do. I promise it will be in good hands."

I glanced at Trevor, then back at Alan. "It's really expensive to run an Inn like this. What makes you think you can do any better than my granddad?"

"I don't think we can do it better, but we're young and motivated, and we've got three kids who are getting old enough to help out. It's been a dream of ours for a while to do something like this. I don't suppose there is anything I could say to convince your grandpa that this is a great opportunity for all of us."

"I'm not sure."

"Well, think about it. We're not in any hurry."

191

I nodded and said goodbye, then wrapped my fingers around Trevor's to lead him off the porch. We crossed the parking lot and entered the forest behind his house. I chose one of the longest trails to the peak of the mountain because I wanted to spend as much time with him as possible.

"He sounds like a good buyer," Trevor said.

"Yeah, I guess."

"How are you feeling about all that?"

"Well, I know it's inevitable, but I don't want to move away."

He nodded, as if he could relate. Then he changed the subject as we switch-backed through the trees. "How are you feeling after last night?"

"Okay, considering." I hopped over some fallen logs that blocked the trail. "How's Kailyn?"

"She's still upset and won't talk about it." He took the lead. It had been so long since we'd hiked together, I forgot how fast he moved.

I ran to catch up. "Is it all right if I ask you a question?"

"Yup."

"If a guy likes a girl, what might be a reason why he wouldn't ask her out?"

He looked back over his shoulder and his eyebrows pulled together before he faced forward again. "He could be worried the girl doesn't feel the same way. Maybe he's afraid to get rejected."

"What if he knows for sure she feels the same way?"

"Maybe she already has a boyfriend."

"What if she's single?"

"Maybe the timing isn't right."

I scrambled over a boulder. "How do people know when the timing is right?"

"It just feels right." He stopped to wait for me.

"What if it does feel right?"

He shrugged and continued walking. "The timing has to be right for both people. Maybe there are things they both need to focus on and accomplish before they make a commitment to each other. Maybe they have some growing up they need to do."

That comment hit me hard. I was the one who had some growing up to do. The problem was, if he kept travelling and experiencing amazing things without me, I would never be able to lessen the gap between us. "What if they could be together and still accomplish all those things?"

He slowed down a little as we edged along a narrow, steep part of the trail. "If they're friends he may not want to ruin the friend-ship."

"Oh." It hadn't occurred to me that if a romantic relationship with him didn't work out, our friendship would be lost too. That would suck. I sighed and hiked quietly for a while. "Did you meet lots of girls in Europe?"

"Yup."

"Did you like any of them?"

"Some of them were all right."

"Have you ever been in love?"

"Once." He turned his head to look back at me again. "Did you love Steve?"

"No." I took a deep breath and prepared myself to be honest. "I love someone else."

He nodded as if it was an interesting fact, but he didn't say anything. He traversed along a fallen tree without looking at me.

"Did you love Corrine Andrews?"

"What?" He stopped abruptly, turned around on the trunk, and stared at me.

"She insinuated you two had been, uh, intimate."

He shook his head. "She's such a liar. We kissed once at a school dance when she was in grade eight and I was in grade nine."

"Who were you in love with?" I pressed.

He took a bottle of water out of his backpack and handed it to me, then took out another one for himself. I watched as he twisted the lid off, drank, and tightened the lid back on. Instead of answering my question, he said, "Whoever this guy is you love, he's not going to want to be a rebound after what Steve did."

I drank some water, then handed him my bottle to put it back in the pack. "What do you mean?"

"You're coming off a relationship with a boyfriend who cheated on you. If the guy really likes you, he'll want to wait until you've recovered."

"Steve cheated because I wasn't that into him, and I was dodging him like a coward for weeks. It's as much my fault as it is his."

"Don't you want your relationship with this other guy to last?"

"Yes."

"Then maybe you should have a rebound relationship with someone else." He started hiking again. I hurried to keep up with him.

"That is the worst advice I've ever heard. I don't want to have a relationship with someone else."

"Any guy in his right mind is going to stay away from you for a while."

"So, you're saying I'm damaged goods because I dated a guy who couldn't keep it in his pants."

He laughed. "You're not damaged goods. It's just that guys get screwed when they date a girl who was treated badly by her previous boyfriend."

"That's bullshit!"

"Don't kill the messenger. I'm just telling you how it is."

"He didn't treat me badly. And I don't see why I should be punished because Steve slept with Lisa."

"Don't worry about it. If the guy loves you he'll wait for as long as it takes." He reached his arm out and took my hand to help me step on the rocks to cross a stream. We got to a difficult part of the hike where we had to use anchored chains to maneuver up a crevice and along a narrow ridge. We had to cross a series of metal ladders that bridged the gaps between rock faces. When we got close to the top of the mountain, the terrain got easier again, so I continued our conversation.

"How long would a guy normally wait before asking out a girl who is supposedly recovering from being scorned?"

"Depends."

"Depends on what?"

We reached the peak and he still hadn't answered. I sat down on the rock and looked out at the view. He sat down beside me and pulled out two granola bars from his pack. He handed me one.

"Depends on what?" I repeated.

"Did you sleep with Steve?"

"That's kind of a personal question, don't you think?"

"Sorry. You don't have to answer it."

"Why do you want to know?"

He shook his head and stared out at the view. "It's none of my business. I shouldn't have asked. Sorry."

"I didn't. That's why he slept with Lisa. I'm a prude and a tease and still pathetically inexperienced. I was a horrible girlfriend."

It looked like maybe he smiled, but I couldn't quite tell because he turned his head away from me. He held out a piece of granola for a chipmunk that scurried around us. It scrambled up the rock and extended its front paws up to take the granola out of Trevor's hand. Then it ran off and disappeared back into the trees. "You weren't a horrible girlfriend. You were there for him after his sister died. He was lucky to have you."

I nodded, reminded of how Trevor had done the same for me. "I tried to support Steve the way you supported me after my dad died. It was way harder than you made it look, and I don't think I ever thanked you back then. So, thank you."

"You're welcome." He turned his hat the right way around and pulled it low to shade his eyes from the sun.

We used to hike to the same spot with our dads nearly every weekend when we were young. Then, as we got older, we explored the ridges on our own. I was never afraid of anything when we were together. As I stared at him, I was reminded of that comfort.

"Memories of your dad don't live in the Inn. They'll live in your heart even if the Inn gets sold or torn down. You know that, right?"

I inhaled and smiled because it felt good to have someone know me as well as Trevor did. "It's not just the memories. I feel him there. He's in the kitchen making a sandwich late at night when I get a glass of milk. He's sitting in the library reading a book by the fire when I come home from school and it's stormy outside. He's in his room shining his boots. I can smell his after-shave. I can hear his laugh. I can feel him kiss my forehead before I fall asleep."

Trevor glanced sideways at me and smiled sympathetically. "He'll be with you no matter where you go. He's not hanging out at the Inn. He's hanging out with you."

I hoped my expression clearly showed my other reason for wanting to stay in Britannia. "I still don't want to leave."

"Well, you're going to have to at some point. Both of us are."

It sounded kind of callous, but it was true.

When I didn't respond, he opened the pack and pulled out an apple. He bit off a chunk and gave it to the chipmunk. After it ran away, Trevor finished the apple and stood. "Ready to go to the springs?"

I stood and reluctantly followed him back towards the forest. "So, is there no way I could convince the guy I love to ask me out right away?"

He chuckled, as if he'd hoped we were done with the conversation but wasn't surprised I hadn't let it go. "You should probably focus on school and getting your scholarship."

"I can do that and have a boyfriend at the same time. I had

a boyfriend this year, his sister died, and you abandoned me, but I still worked really hard to catch up on my assignments and got straight A's."

He stopped abruptly and turned to face me, his expression etched with pain. "I didn't abandon you. I would never abandon you."

It was a trigger for him because of his mom, but it was true, so I laid it out. "You left me for five months."

"You left for a year," he snapped and spun around to keep walking.

"That was different." I ran to keep up because he started moving at the speed he would use if he were on a rescue. "Trevor, I'm not blaming you. I'm just saying it was hard."

"It was hard for me too," he said without looking at me.

Okay. What did that mean, exactly? I grabbed his elbow to make him turn around. "You know who the guy I love is, right?"

He stared at me in a way that reminded me of when we were little. For a fraction of a second, he looked like the little boy I had spent pretty much every waking minute with. He inhaled and his expression shifted back to his serious adult face. "Do you trust him?"

"With my life." I leaned back against a tree trunk.

He stepped forward until our cheeks were touching and whispered, "Then trust him. If it's meant to be, you can get together with him when the timing is right."

He turned and disappeared down the path that led to the Britannia pools. My legs got weak, partly from the promise of what he said and partly from the disappointment of having to wait. I had to sit on the ground to recover. If his idea was to make me wait just so I would want him even more, it was working.

Eventually, I got up and made my way to the hot springs. It consisted of a series of seven natural pools of hot spring water that tiered down the mountain like stepping stones. It was a nice day, so all the pools were packed with people. Trevor was already talking to a group of his Search and Rescue buddies, so I sat down on a boulder and texted Sophie: *911. Where are you?*

Just parked at the pools. Come over.

Already here. Need to consult re: Trevor. ASAP.

Two minutes later, she and Doug found me. He went to join Trevor and Murphy. Sophie and I climbed up to our favourite boulder above the top pool. We always tanned on it because it stayed sunny all day, and it was the best spot to see and be seen from.

"Don't," I warned her when I noticed a group of younger girls already set up on our spot. "We can sit on the other side."

Sophie turned and raised her eyebrow at me, determined. As we got closer, the girls saw Sophie and quickly gathered up their towels and bags before scrambling to the boulder on the other side.

"Thanks," I sang cheerfully to the girls who vacated the spot. "You're a menace," I mumbled to Sophie.

"What? I throw a girl off a cliff into the pool one time two years ago, and now everyone respects me. That is not my fault."

"They don't respect you. They're scared of you."

"Same difference. I've been extremely well behaved lately."

"You jumped off the stage and threatened Lisa Alvarez last night," I reminded her as I rolled the towels out for us to sit on.

"Oh yeah, right. She deserved it. What's the deal with Trevor?"

I stripped down to my bathing suit and borrowed some of her sunscreen. "He doesn't want to date until the timing is right, whatever that means. He also suggested I have a rebound relationship to get over Steve. I think. It's hard to know for sure. We were speaking in hypotheticals."

"Why weren't you speaking in real-life-theticals?"

"Good question. I guess if I'm too chicken to talk openly about a relationship with him, I'm obviously still too immature to have one with him." I sighed at the realization that he was right to want to wait.

"Hi Derian." I heard a cartoony voice behind me.

I turned my head and smiled. "Hey Niko."

He climbed up onto the boulder and sat on a log. He wasn't wearing his glasses and his hair, wet from swimming, was slicked back off his face. "Mason says you might want to be my tutor while he's gone."

"Sure. I would love to. What do you mean by gone?"

"He's going away to work for his dad in a bunch of different countries around the world."

Sophie abruptly stood up behind us and yelled, "Hey Alvarez! Does your mom know how much of a slut you are? I'd be happy to tell her when she comes into the salon to get her roots done."

Nikolai and I both leaned forward over the edge of the boulder.

"The next time you drop your panties to whore yourself, make sure it's with a guy who doesn't have a girlfriend."

Lisa shouted back, "Maybe if the girlfriend knew how to satisfy her man he wouldn't have come crawling to me begging for it."

"We all know he didn't have to beg for it since you give it away for free." Sophie picked up a handful of rocks and chucked them at Lisa. "Leave." Lisa jumped around to avoid getting hit. Everyone laughed at her. "I just had a manicure done," Sophie shouted. "Don't make me come down there."

Lisa grabbed her bag and climbed awkwardly down the boulders, then disappeared into the forest. Two of her friends shot Sophie a glaring look before they followed behind Lisa.

"She scares me," Nikolai whispered to me as he stared at Sophie.

"Was that really necessary?" I asked her as she sat back down.

"No, just entertaining." She leaned back on her elbows.

Nikolai scooted past Sophie as if he thought she was going to lash out at him. "I'm going tell Mason you agreed to be my tutor."

"He's here?" I asked.

"Yeah, right there." Nikolai pointed to the boulder right below ours. "I'll see you later." He jumped into the pool and swam over to talk to Mason, then he pointed up at me. Mason smiled and climbed up to join me. He moved awkwardly because his knee brace wasn't cooperating. He wasn't wearing a shirt, and a small tattoo was visible on the upper part of his left chest. It had the letters CC and a series of numbers with dashes in between. At first, I thought it looked like a military tattoo, but then I realized it was initials and a date. The year was the same year my dad died.

"Hey, how's it going?" he asked.

"Good. Thanks. How are you?"

"The bum knee is a pain, but I'm fine. Thanks."

I nodded, still wondering the significance of his tattoo. "Nikolai mentioned you're leaving."

"Yeah. My dad lined up an internship for me in his international division until next summer. Do you mind being Niko's tutor while I'm gone?"

"I'd be happy to. When do you leave?"

"The day after tomorrow."

"Oh, so soon. Cool. Well, it was nice meeting you. Too bad we didn't get to know each other better over the school year."

He leaned back to sit on a rock and grinned. "Yeah. I wish Steve would have screwed up a long time ago."

What? "Really?"

"Definitely. Is it all right if I make you a deal?"

I nodded, curious what it was.

"When I come back, if you're single, I'd like to ask you out on a date. If you're interested."

Uh, yeah, I was definitely interested if things didn't develop with Trevor. But I might be living in Vancouver by the time he got back. Or not. A lot could change. There were no guarantees where I would be or what I'd be doing. If we were both single and living in close proximity, there was no reason not to say yes. The chances of it happening were slim, and it wasn't as if he was asking me to sign a legally binding contract. "Okay, it's a deal."

He stretched his arm out and shook my hand. "All right, I'll see you in a year." He turned and hobbled back towards the edge of the boulder.

"Hey, are you going to at least come home for a visit at Christmas?" I asked.

He turned and smiled. "No, but maybe Santa will send you another gift."

My eyes opened wide and my mouth dropped open. He winked before he stepped down and disappeared. I spun around to Sophie. "Oh my God. Did you hear that?" I asked her.

"Yeah, you have to wait for both Trevor and Mason. Good job."

"Not that. I think he's the Santa who sent me The Ramones record last Christmas."

"So, he's a crazy stalker?"

I frowned, but before I had a chance to respond, a guy I'd never seen before sat on the log in front of Sophie. He wore board shorts and had tattoos on his shoulders. His dark hair was shaved at the sides in a Mohawk, and he had plug piercings in both ears. He smiled at Sophie, waiting for her to look up at him. "Are all the girls in this bloody awful town as beautiful as you?"

"Watch your mouth. That's my hometown you're calling bloody awful," Sophie quipped.

"Sorry." He grinned. "If all the talent around here is like you I'll upgrade my assessment. What's your name, love?"

"Sophie. And you?"

"Jax."

"Are you visiting?"

"Nope. I just moved here from London. I heard there's a band that's somewhat tolerable playing Saturday night at some old railroad station. Wanna go with me, Sophie?"

She glanced at me and grinned. "I'm actually in the band that's somewhat tolerable, so I'm going to already be there. This would probably be a good time for me to mention that my boyfriend is also in the band."

Jax clutched his chest dramatically as if he'd just been shot in the heart. "No. Don't say you have a boyfriend."

"Sorry." She jutted her thumb in my direction. "Derian is recently single if you're looking for a date."

I glared at her. He winked at me and smiled. "I assume that girl you were stoning earlier was involved in the reason Derian is recently single," he said to Sophie.

She shrugged. "She deserved it. She shouldn't have messed with Derian."

He nodded and pressed his lips together as if he were impressed. "What do ya say?" he asked me.

"What?"

"Do ya wanna go out?"

I looked over at Sophie. She smiled in *why the hell not* way. He was cute. More Sophie's type than mine, but he seemed pretty cool. I had a feeling if I had a rebound fling with him, Trevor was going to hate that he was tatted up and pierced. Even though there was a part of me that wanted to make Trevor regret his suggestion to have a rebound, I needed to act like an adult, not an adolescent. "No thank you. I'm in love with someone, so it wouldn't be fair to you."

He laughed. "All right. If you change your mind, I'll be around."

Sophie grinned and pointed over my shoulder. Doug, Murphy, and Trevor were all climbing up towards the boulder we were sitting on.

Jax laughed. It sounded more nervous than he probably wanted it to. "Cheers." He waved and did a back flip off the opposite side of the boulder. Sophie and I both lunged forward and peered over the edge to make sure he landed safely in the pool below. He popped up through the surface of the water with a mischievous grin.

"Who was that?" Trevor asked.

"Derian's future rebound." Sophie laughed. "He's bad-assed and will definitely be trouble."

Murphy and Doug's expressions seemed intrigued. Trevor frowned at me. "Can I talk to you?"

"Sure." I grabbed my clothes, scrambled to my feet, and followed him into the forest. I thought for sure he was going to tell me he changed his mind. I waited for him to say he wanted me to be his girlfriend, but he didn't. He looked mad, furious actually.

"Did you contact my mom?"

My stomach clenched, and my heart felt like it stopped beating. "Uh, not exactly."

"What exactly did you do?"

"I found out her phone number and gave it to Kailyn."

He stepped back, his jaw tensed, the veins in his temples bulging.

I stepped into my shorts and pulled them up over my hips. "She was really sad while you were gone. She begged me to get it for her."

"God damn it, Derian. I specifically told you not to do that."

"She's an adult. She has a right to talk to her mom if she wants to."

"You think so? My dad just called. Kailyn finally told him the reason she's been crying is because Lorraine told her she didn't want her to call ever again."

"Oh my God. I'm so sorry." My stomach twisted with guilt. "I didn't know your mom was going to be unreceptive."

"Yeah, well, Lorraine is a self-absorbed bitch, Deri. What did you think would happen? She didn't want a daughter with special needs, or a simple, blue-collared husband, or a son who reminded her of her responsibilities, or a small-town life she felt trapped in. She wanted to be free to live all over the world, entertain herself with a rotating door of rich and sophisticated men, and never be accountable to anyone." He paced as the years of buried anger surfaced. "It would take hours to tell you all the selfish things she's done. Bottom line: she didn't love us. And Kailyn deserves better than that."

I opened my mouth to respond, but he held up his hand to stop me.

"I told you there were things you don't know. You should have trusted me."

I was stunned, partly by the truth and partly by the fact he hadn't confided in me before. "You've never, I didn't, I'm sorr—"

"Don't bother. I don't want to hear it." He turned and stormed away.

Completely crushed by the regret of exposing Kailyn to something that caused her pain, I said goodbye to everyone and hiked back alone. I should have respected Trevor's wishes, but in fairness, it would have been easier if he had trusted me enough to be open and tell me about his mom and the things she had done. I wasn't perfect but neither was he.

Regardless, there was no denying that the universe had spoken, and what it said—loud and clear—was I was destined to be single. The signs all pointed to me needing to focus on my personal development for a while. Alone. Independent.

Who was I to argue with the universe? Presumably, everything would work out the way it was supposed to. Whether I would like the end result or not was to be determined.

When I arrived back at the Inn, Granddad was sitting in the library, reading. I sat on the arm of his chair and sighed. "Is it all right if we talk for a few minutes?"

"Of course." He closed his book and rested it on his lap, ready to listen.

"I met the man who wants to buy the Inn. He and his family sound like a great match. If that's what you want to do, I'd be happy with that."

"Well, thank you for saying so, but I realized I wouldn't know what to do with myself if I wasn't running this place. I told him I wasn't quite ready to retire yet. Since he's not in any hurry, he's going to check back next spring. If you don't mind helping me out every morning, we can definitely stay until you finish high school." He patted my hand. "What do you think of that idea?"

So relieved. I hugged him. "I love that idea."

As I thought about the year that lay ahead for all of us, I moved to sit in my dad's old favourite chair. I ran my finger over the rough leather. Then, just to be sure the universe and Trevor both knew my intentions, I pulled out my phone and put it out there: *To be clear, you are the person I trust. With my life. Always.*

The End Of Book One.

ACKNOWLEDGEMENTS

None of my books would be possible without the support of my husband Sean and the rest of my family. Thank you to my critique partner Denise Jaden, my muse for this series John Hughes, Greg Ng (and the moms from his class who volunteered to read a very early rough draft of this story), Rasadi Cortes, Erica Ediger, Jen Wilson, Belinda Wagner, Lisa Marks, Cory Cavazzi, my mom and dad, my brother Rob, my sister Luan, my editors Charlotte Ledger and Laura McCallen, and the entire team behind the scenes at Harper*Impulse* and HarperCollins*Publishers*. I'd also like to send a special thank-you to the real Search and Rescue volunteers and first responders in the Squamish area, and the young adult bloggers and youth librarians who tirelessly introduce books to young readers.